Deadly Questions

A Jamie Pellen Mystery

Deadly Questions

A Jamie Pellen Mystery

Princess Palmer

Writers Club Press
San Jose New York Lincoln Shanghai

Deadly Questions
A Jamie Pellen Mystery

Writers Club Press
an imprint of iUniverse.com, Inc.

For information address:
iUniverse.com, Inc.
5220 S 16th, Ste. 200
Lincoln, NE 68512
www.iuniverse.com

The setting, characters, and events in this mystery are totally fictional.

ISBN: 0-595-16506-0

Printed in the United States of America

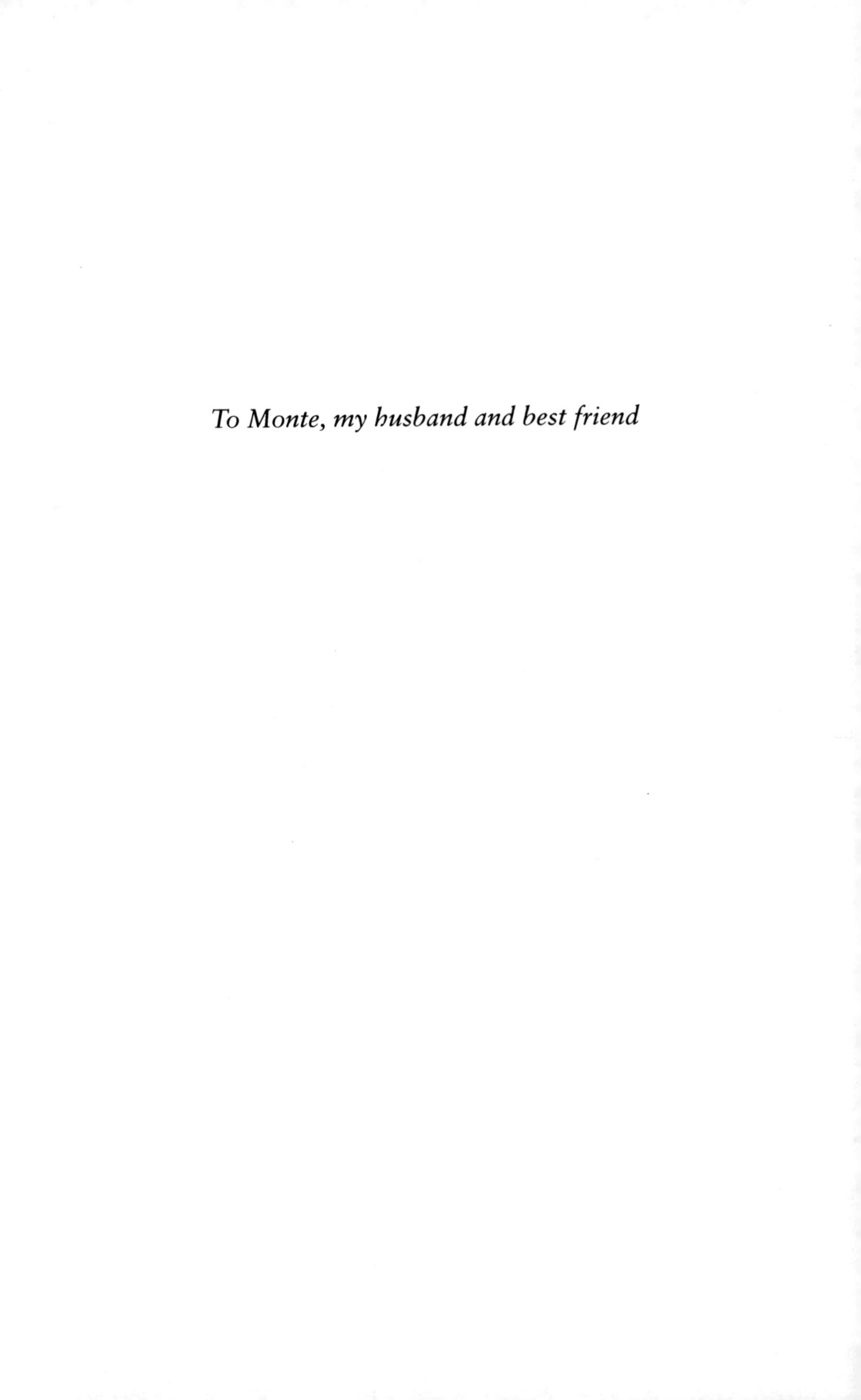

To Monte, my husband and best friend

Acknowledgements

This book could not have been completed without the ideas and encouragement from Deputy Sheriff Leslie Kitching and Kathie Austin. A special thank you also to Sarah Ducharme for editing the manuscript.

I

The lemony light of the sunrise peeked through the limbs of the majestic live oak trees that shaded the dog kennel. The temperature in Brookdale was already 85 degrees with 90% humidity. The small town was located in Dora County on the Florida/Georgia border.

Jamie turned to the dogs and said, "Good morning, babies. How did everyone sleep last night?" The dogs barked and whined in response to Jamie's greeting.

Jamie Pellen's upscale dog-boarding kennel was about one-fourth full. Business at the end of August was slow. Just ten of the fifty kennels were occupied, so Jamie's daily chores did not take long. She hosed down the kennels, filled up the water bowls as country music blared from the built-in stereo system.

Jamie's own Black Lab, Major and her Aussie Shepherd, Minor, were allowed out to run around the exercise pen with the other dogs while she cleaned up. Major, her 14-year old lover-dog moved a little slow now, but he still had a ferocious bark. Minor, her pal, went everywhere with Jamie and was seldom out of arms reach.

"Ja-a-im-ee! Ja-a-im-ee!" Fred called. He could make her 2-syllable name into four, sometimes.

"I'm in the kennel," Jamie yelled back. She looked over at the kennel entrance as he entered. Fred was a lean 6'4", bald as a peanut and had the most captivating baby blue eyes that appeared to look right through you to your most inner thoughts. His year 'round tan gave him an eternal youthful appearance. He credited his exercise program and moderation in eating for his excellent health at age 56.

His regime was contagious. Once a couch potato, Jamie had changed her eating habits and had begun to exercise when she and Fred began dating. As a result, Jamie had acquired the same glowing youthful appearance. She had short bouncy brown hair, and intense hazel green eyes. She was 5'10" and 10 years Fred's junior.

Uh-oh. Jamie thought. She knew that look too well…the slight grin, the sparkle in the eyes…a look that meant he had received an invitation for an adventure. "What?" Jamie asked eagerly.

"Want to go to Egypt?" Fred asked looking at her with those gorgeous baby blues.

"Who's paying?" Jamie asked.

"CRT."

"What's CRT?"

"A Washington consulting firm. Sue Bolds was the lady I spoke with. She said The World Bank had referred me. CRT wants to know if I am available to go to Egypt to head a research project for their firm. We would need to be in Cairo for a month. What do you think? Are you game?"

"When?"

"If we left the second week in September, we'd be back at the beginning of October."

"Oh-h-h, Fred. Em won't be back until the second week in September. She's so good with the dogs and taking care of the business. I don't know anyone else that I would trust. Could we go after she gets back?"

"The problem is that they want the survey completed, compiled and analyzed by the first of the year. Why don't I go over on the first and then you join me when Em gets back?"

"That sounds good except I don't know if she will be available. I can't reach her because she's sunning herself on some beach in Mexico. Besides, by the time I got to Egypt, you'd be about ready to come back."

Jamie looked at Fred. She hated to be away from him and he knew it. They had agreed upon a maximum of three weeks apart when they were married. Fred usually held to this agreement. She knew he needed the stimulus he got out of conducting research but most of all, he really enjoyed visiting the Middle East. His love for the diverse culture and the warm, friendly people of the area had resulted in extended visits to the area.

"No, I'll still have two weeks, and you can help with the project if you want," Fred suggested.

"Okay, but I am going to be terribly lonely until I can join you, and you have to call me everyday." Fred pulled her close and tenderly kissed her.

"I love you so much," Jamie whispered. "Just be careful. I don't want anything to happen to you." Fred walked back to the house to call CRT to accept the contract.

Jamie's mind began to wander as she continued her chores. Her thoughts went back to an extended 2-year visit to Cairo in the early 1980's. She had seen speeding cars and busses hit pedestrians. One incident that stood out in her mind was when a car was speeding down an off ramp. A middle-aged man was crossing a 6-laned major highway. He had made it to the middle and was waiting for a break in the traffic to cross the other three lanes of traffic. His back was to the off ramp. The car sped across the road and hit the man from the back. He flew about 12 feet into the air, across two lanes of traffic, hit the windshield of a car in the third lane and plopped to the ground on the side of the road. The driver of the car did not stop, nor did any traffic. A pedestrian walked over to the injured man and shook his shoulder to see if he was okay but there was no response so he walked off. No one seemed to care.

During the early 80's, cars parked on the broad sidewalks and the people had no choice but to walk among the traffic. There were few stoplights and few traffic controls except during peak hours. The cars would zip around the roads, when there was space to zip, making it the pedestrian's responsibility to get out of the way.

Driving in Cairo was just as much of an adventure as walking. Drivers were responsible for everyone in front of them, thus giving them free reign to make sudden stops, 180 degree U-turns or abrupt right or left turns without a signal. This kept the cars behind them, as well as the unfortunate pedestrians, guessing as to what the driver in front might do. If traffic moved too slowly, drivers just passed everyone in the oncoming lane of mangled traffic. Of course, this brought all traffic to a stand still. Unless, of course, one was fortunate enough to ride from the airport into Cairo proper at 1 am when the streets were a little less congested. Then, the ride was a hair-raising 90-mph race to the hotel.

The traffic situation has changed a lot in Cairo in the sense that the unpredictable traffic flows much more evenly and the cars no longer park on the sidewalks along the corniche beside the Nile. But, Jamie still had visions of the pedestrians being thrown high up into the air and splatting on a busy road. For some reason, she always worried that Fred would get hit and had she been there, she could have prevented it. She dreamed about this while he was away. The Islamic militants and the sporadic bombing of tourist buses should be her major concern now, rather than the chaotic traffic. But, old memories die hard.

Jamie turned to one of her canine guests and said, "Hey, big guy! You look like you need some attention." The Russian Wolfhound arched his back so she could reach all the "good" rubbing spots. Jamie loved operating a boarding kennel.

Jamie and Fred had quit their salaried jobs 5 years ago and had become self-employed. Jamie had worked as an English teacher at Brookdale High School and Fred had taught at Florida State University. Their dream had been to live on acreage where Jamie could run a kennel to board dogs and a place that would serve as a base for Fred to work as a consultant for international firms. They were delighted when they found an isolated 100-acre plot of land with majestic oaks surrounded by a hammock right in Brookdale.

The 100 acres included a somewhat dilapidated horse stable and a old style "Florida" house with its tin roof, large overhangs, high ceilings, a crawl space, a long four foot wide hallway with three rooms on each side, floor to ceiling windows, and a gravel driveway. This style house kept the inside cool in the summer and remained warm in Florida's mild winters.

The horse stable was redesigned into a dog kennel where the guests were pampered. The kennel offered a pick up and delivery service, air conditioning, heating, and piped in music. The competition among boarding kennels was not intense in Dora County. In fact, most boarding kennels in this area stayed fairly full. However, there were nearly 100 kennels in nearby Tallahassee, if you counted all the backyard mini-kennels and the vet's 8-10 cramped pens to house animals. The management quality ranged from very poor where kennel owners placed 2-3 strange dogs together in one run to the plush indoor/outdoor runs with carpet and TV. The distinguishing characteristic of Jamie's kennel was that the dogs were given lots of tender, loving care and a high level of inter-species communication.

As she returned to the house from the kennel, Jamie heard a new mechanical sound, like a large machine, maybe a bulldozer.

She went up to the back door stuck her head inside, and yelled, "Fred, come outside with me for a minute."

He ambled out onto the screened porch. The machinery was still grinding away. They listened for a minute or so. "What do you think that is?" Jamie asked.

"Sounds like someone is clearing the Livingston property. Mike must have sold it."

Mike Livingston had inherited the 5000 acres that joined the Pellen property when his dad had died about six months ago. A plantation of 25,000 acres surrounded the Pellen's 100 acres on the north side, the Livingston property on the west side, national forest on the east side, and the highway on the southern front.

"Let's walk over to the property line and take a peek," Jamie suggested. They walked down the narrow trail which had been cleared through the live oaks, sweet gums, pines, and sumacs. The grinding noise grew louder.

Jamie glanced at Fred's stern face. He was worried. They had moved to the country for tranquility. But, in areas where the land had no restrictions, they always had a fear of what would be built right next to them. They had hoped that 100 acres would keep them pretty well insulated.

They came up to the creek that flowed across the side of Livingston's property and along the Pellen's property line. The yellow Caterpillar bulldozer, with the help of a blue and yellow Kawasaki backhoe was pulling up tree stumps. The trees, which had been cut down, were stacked neatly for the logger's truck. The trees had been separated into two stacks: one of pine and one of hardwoods. A large stump of firelighter was placed next to the pine pile.

"Looks like they are putting through a road. Is that Mark Downing on that backhoe?" asked Fred.

"It does look like him. Let's go see what's happening," Jamie suggested. They jumped the creek and walked out into the clearing. It was Mark. Fred waved at him just as he looked over at the clearing. He put his big Kawasaki backhoe on idle and jumped down.

"Hey, Fred. Jamie. Sorry about the noise," he said with a grin. Mark was the husband of Jamie's buddy, Junith Wilson, the Sheriff of Dora County.

"We just wondered what was happening over here. Are you clearing a road or a super highway?" Fred asked.

Mark looked a little apologetic as he explained, "It's my understanding that they are going to put a paved road through here, heavy enough for 18 wheelers which is like putting in a highway. They're paying big bucks for it, that's for sure. My boss is real excited."

"Do you know anything about these people?" Jamie asked.

"No one has seen them. We got an order with blueprints, permits, and a check to put this road in. It's a mile stretch back to the cleared pasture acreage."

"We'll let you get back to work. Stop over for a cold beer when you get finished for the day," Fred offered.

"We won't quit until about 10 tonight. I know you guys are early to bed. Maybe another day." They watched as Mark got up into his machine. He was good at what he did. He could make that machine pluck a tree out of a dense forest while everything else was left totally undisturbed.

Mark was very much a conservationist. He had refused to clear a wooded area with a cocated woodpecker's nest and once defied his boss by clearing around a tree with an osprey's nest in it. He appreciated nature and did his part to help the natural wildlife survive.

"Wonder who bought that land and why all the secrecy?" Jamie asked.

"I don't know but they sure seem to be in a hurry. Out of the 5000 acres, there is a sink hole nearly 500 feet wide, 1,000 cleared acres and the rest is heavily wooded. We are about 200 miles from any major city. That doesn't add up to an ideal corporate sight in my book. We'll need to keep a close eye on this quasi-secret operation. I'm sorry I'm going to be gone next month. This project is going to develop very quickly."

The Pellens had discovered that County guidelines were fairly adequate when used to prevent certain undesirable development but they were useless in removing anything once it had been developed on the sly, so to speak. Thus, to make a difference, they had to somehow squelch this project early if indeed it were an undesirable one, or at least delay it until they could figure out what was going on.

Fred and Jamie walked back to their house. "Let me put the soup on and then we'll take a walk while it's cooking," Jamie said. She stopped to pick some habanera peppers and mint from the plush garden. Jamie's green thumb had produced a hedge of peppers ranging from sweet yellow banana peppers to orange habanera peppers. A border of parsley, basil, sage and oregano surrounded the pepper bushes. In the middle was a lemon tree loaded with unripe fruit almost pulling the limbs to the ground. The lemon tree was a special hybrid that could withstand the cool north Florida temperatures.

Jamie fixed some of Fred's favorite soup for supper. It was a special recipe she had learned from a Libyan friend. In Arabic it is called *sherba* which means soup. It is a tasty, spicy soup with lamb and vegetables. The tomato-based broth was flavored with onions, cumin and turmeric.

Fred sat in the kitchen and chatted while Jamie chopped the onions, potatoes, zucchini, yellow squash, green beans and opened a can of garbanzos. Once the lamb and onions had been sautéed in the spices, she had added the veggies.

"It will mess up everything if the wrong type of business goes up over there. Our property value could drop severely," he predicted with knitted brow.

"You know we cannot do anything about whatever develops on that property. We'll just have to accept it. We can't buy up the whole county."

Her words were not very convincing but she had tried to make Fred feel better. He had not wanted neighbors, period. That was one aspect that had sold them on this land: the fact that their nearest neighbors were 5 miles away.

"I don't mind some development. I just wish I knew what it was. Ray Livingston was a nice guy. He never would have sold that land. He loved it. He used to hunt and fish there every weekend. His son, however, is just a money grubber. I knew he'd sell it after Ray died. He probably sold it cheap or lost it in a poker game."

Jamie finished preparing the soup by adding the water and left it to simmer. Fred grabbed his .38 and recommended that they wear their snake boots. The snake boots were made of kevlar, the same material as a bullet-proof vest. Rattlesnakes could not bite through it. Due to the extremely dry weather, the snakes were on the move. They seemed to be on the move most of the time, as far as Jamie could tell. They moved when it was dry to find water and they moved when it was wet to get out of the water.

"What exactly will you be doing in Egypt?" Jamie asked, hoping to get his mind off the road development.

"Remember the study on bureaucracy I did about 15 years ago? CRT wants me to replicate it to see if the changes that were made then have been effective over the years. It could prove to be very interesting." They walked in comfortable silence for about 10 minutes.

"Are you going by to see Mother today?" Fred asked.

"I'm going to wait until you leave then go see her. She called yesterday to complain about her food and roommate. I'd better go see what's up," Jamie replied.

Fred's mother had been in a nursing home for the past five years. While her 95 year old body was shrunken and failing due to arthritis and old age, her mind was as bright and sharp as ever. Fred found it extremely painful to see his mother in that state of being. He used to visit her once per week, as a dutiful son should. The last few months, however, he found it too painful.

"Stop!" Jamie said softly as she firmly grabbed Fred's arm. "Look up ahead about 20 feet."

Stretched out across the path was a water moccasin. Fred pulled out his .38, stepped a little closer and fired. That would be one less worry in their lives.

Fred and Jamie were both nature lovers. They respected most of the critters that walked, flew or slithered across their property. The only one that they felt compelled to kill was the water moccasin or cotton mouth moccasin as it is sometimes called. These snakes were aggressors. They attack and were dangerous. It was the only real danger they worried about in their woods.

Rattlesnakes were often thought to be dangerous but they generally did not bother people and would run away when given the chance. Jamie had even come as close as one foot away from a coiled, rattling rattler and he had not attempted to strike. Her heart, on the other hand, almost stopped. But water moccasins were different.

"Well, this has not turned into a relaxing walk," Jamie said.

"Let's go ahead and walk the trail and then eat. I'm getting hungry."

They walked the 3 mile circuit of their cleared trail in the forest. It had been a hard job to make this trail but it was well worth it. The five foot swaths through the mesic hammock took them through a mixture of southern magnolias, laurel oaks, popcorn trees, swamp chestnut oaks, live oaks, water oaks, dogwoods, grape vines, ferns, pine trees, wild azaleas and blueberry bushes. These plants make homes for birds such as the Blue Jay, Tufted Titmouse, the Red-bellied Woodpecker, Piliated Woodpecker, Cardinals, Downy Woodpecker, Blue-Gray Gnatcatcher, Giant Crested Fly-Catcher, Barred Owls, bats, Carolina Chickadees, Red Winged Hawks and seasonal red-winged blackbirds and cedar waxwings.

"Jamie, look!" Up ahead were five huge wild turkeys. Once they noticed Fred and Jamie, and they began to fly away. The flapping wings were thunderous. They sounded like 747's taking off. It was wonderful.

Fred took Jamie's hand in his and said, "That's what I don't want messed up out here. I don't want anything to disturb the wildlife or the habitat that we have." They walked back to the house in thoughtful silence.

The fragrance of cumin, lamb and mint filled their nostrils when they entered the kitchen. "Smells great," Fred said.

Fred answered the phone while Jamie dished up the steaming, spicy sherba. She topped each bowl with chopped fresh mint and squeezed in some lemon juice.

"Who was that?" Jamie asked.

"Suzanne from CRT. She said I would have my ticket for Cairo by Monday. I will leave on Tuesday."

"Tuesday? That's day after tomorrow." Jamie always agreed to these trips until they actually happened. Then she would become very moody and lonely, even if it were just for two weeks until she would join him.

Being left alone always caused Jamie to be moody. She isolated herself from her friends, would forget to eat, and didn't sleep. It came from never having been alone as a child or even as a young adult. She worked hard to overcome the trauma of being alone and had conquered most of her fears.

"I don't have to go if you don't want me to," Fred offered.

"Right."

He knew she wouldn't back out now. Tears filled her eyes. "I just don't like being without you." Fred held her close.

"Why not come along now? Linda could come stay at the house and manage the kennel for you. The Cairo hotels are nice. You could read and shop. The embassy folks are always looking for bridge players. Come go with me."

"My, that sure sounds exciting," Jamie said in her best sarcastic voice. "No, Linda could keep the kennel but she doesn't really like dogs. Emily is out-of-town until the 15th of September. I would feel better about it if we waited. Guess I'll just have to be lonely."

2

Tuesday came too quickly. Fred's plane was to leave at 3:30 p.m. Jamie spent the morning washing, ironing and helping him pack.

"Let's leave for the airport at 1:00. I want to stop at the bank for some cash and have time to have some coffee with you before I take off," Fred said.

Tears filled Jamie's eyes, once again.

"Come here, you goose," he said as he took her in his arms. "You can still come with me."

The tears gushed until Fred held her close and led her to the bed. He lay down beside her and softly whispered, "I love you Jay Jay. What's wrong?"

"I just hate it when you're gone," Jamie managed to gulp out between sobs. Jamie really felt like an immature kid but his leaving just hurt so badly. It was a prelude to the loneliness she was about to have to face.

"I know. It won't be so long. I'll see you in 15 short days."

"OK." She tried to smile. She knew she must have looked beautiful with a red blotched face and swollen eyes. She got up and took a shower.

The nearest airport was in Tallahassee, about 35 minutes from their house in Brookdale. On the way, they stopped at the bank.

"Now, I don't want you to do anything stupid while I'm gone," Fred ordered.

"Oh, come on Fred. Sometimes you treat me like a child." Jamie smiled and added, "Just because I act like one once in while is no reason."

She had done some stupid things when Fred was out of town. Again, it went back to the "moody & lonely" syndrome.

Her women libber friends hated it when Jamie said she believed that loneliness and moodiness was not just a female thing. Rather, it was the result of feeling defenseless. Women were just more vulnerable than men and must compensate for this vulnerability through precautions like security systems, training in the martial arts, and knowing how to handle guns. While Jamie rejected the martial arts, she did have a security system and several guns.

"Really. Make sure you turn on both the kennel security system and the system in the house," Fred instructed.

"I will. They make me feel a lot safer," Jamie admitted.

"If one goes off, let the dogs out and get a gun." She glanced over at Fred and with a sparkle in her eye, and responded quickly.

"What do you mean let the dogs out? You know I don't let the dogs in the house when you are gone." She looked at him with complete sweetness and innocence.

"Yeah, right. Then why are there always fleas in the house when I get back from a trip overseas?"

"You must bring them back with you."

"Jamie, I'm serious. Don't go outside if you think someone is out there. And, if the alarm is going off when you come home, leave immediately. Don't get out of the car. I mean it. Nothing in the house is worth your life," he said as he touched her knee.

Jamie dropped him off at the terminal and parked the car. They met in the coffee shop. They sat close to each other but didn't talk much. When it was time to go, she was brave. She kissed him goodbye and watched him as he boarded the plane. She didn't break out into tears until she was inside the truck. Jamie sat there and cried until she saw his plane takeoff then wiped her eyes.

3

Jamie spent the rest of the day and the next morning in the kennel. She cleaned and exercised her guests. After an afternoon of intense energy release, she was relaxed enough to call Vonnie, Fred's mother.

"Hello," answered a weak, frail voice.

"Hi, it's Jamie."

"Yeah?" She answered as if her busy day had been rudely interrupted.

"Would you like to go to lunch on Thursday?" Jamie asked.

"No, I don't feel good," she answered.

"Okay. I'll see you tomorrow about 11:00. We'll see how you feel then," Jamie suggested.

"Okay."

"Bye, bye," Jamie said and hung up the phone. She shook her head. Vonnie never felt like going out. Nursing homes were not the best place for active minds but were necessary for incapacitated bodies. Too bad there was no place for an active mind.

Being alone in the rural south was lonely but it was also very peaceful. Fred had called last night, but after a day of just her and the dogs, Jamie had had enough quiet time. She had turned down various invitations to have dinner with friends. She forced herself to call Junith. "Want to go out to the shooting range this afternoon?" she asked.

"Sure. Indoors or outdoors?" asked Junith.

"Let's try the indoor range. I've never been there," Jamie replied.

"I'll meet you there in 30 minutes."

Jamie placed her .38, .45, 9 mm, and a few rounds of ammo for each gun, ear plugs and eye guards in a gun sack. Minor walked out to the Dodge truck with her and jumped in as soon as she opened the door. Jamie once saw a truck back-end another truck with a Rottweiler riding in the back. The dog flew off the back of the truck, landed on the windshield of the Honda that had followed too close behind the truck. A little deja vu with Cairo. A law was recently passed that required all dogs to be secured when riding in the back of the truck. This was written to protect passers by from getting attacked but also protected the dogs from flying out of the truck bed. Too bad there's not a law to keep children secured in the back of trucks.

About five miles down Highway 20 is a group of houses on two to five acres each. Eddie and Tammie were Jamie's nearest neighbors. They lived in a red brick house with a shiny tin roof, dairy cows in his fenced backyard, Pitbulls in the fenced front yard and a chicken coop in the side yard. He and Tammie were just going out to his truck. Jamie pulled in the driveway. "Hey, Eddie, Tammie. How y'all doin?" Eddie was almost 5'9", flabby, pot-bellied, with black hair and beard, and was always dressed in jeans and a T-shirt, even in the dead of winter.

"Hey, Jamie. Good. Heard from Fred yet?" Eddie asked. Fred had called Eddie the night before he left to let him know to keep an eye on the place since he was the nearest neighbor.

"Yeah. He called last night. He says it is hot over there."

Tammie, his wife, looked over and nodded. She was bone thin with pasty skin, deep socketed pale green eyes and long stringy red hair. She had worked at the Brookdale post office for the past 3 years. She stood quietly next to Eddie as he talked.

"Did you hear that someone bought the Livingston property?" Eddie asked.

"Yes, but I'm not clear on who bought it," Jamie responded.

"Some big corporation is going to farm it is what I heard," Eddie replied.

"Huh. Well, it's not the worst thing that could happen." Jamie smiled but she thought to herself that she did not move to the country to live next to a corporate farm.

"Well, maybe it's just an investment and they won't mess it up too much."

"I hope so." Jamie waved goodbye. Eddie was such a pleasant neighbor. You would never guess that he used to get drunk and beat his first wife and children. They would take refuge with her family during his drunken binges. She finally took the kids and left after 15 years of the abuse. That sobered him up, but not before he lost his job at the gunpowder factory and was discharged from the National Guard. Now he made his living selling milk, eggs and chickens, as well as doing odd jobs. He had helped turn the horse stable into a kennel. He seemed to be adjusting to his new life with Tammie. They had only been married a little over two years.

As she drove down Highway 20 to the shooting range, she passed the trailer parks and lower income subdivisions that were interspersed with shacks and shanties. There were also several small, wooden, decaying churches set up on concrete bricks and surrounded by graveyards. This area was full of rednecks, poor white trash, low income blue gums, corn farms, and cattle ranches. In addition, there was a group of retirees who had bought large pieces of unspoiled land to start home businesses. Most of the land was zoned agricultural which was like not being zoned at all. The advantage was a tremendous tax break if you actually farmed the land or produced something that you could sell, legally. The nice part about living in the country is that anything goes. One could do almost anything on the property without interference from neighbors. Part of the price of this freedom was that one was obliged to ignore what the neighbors did. This was the hard part of the bargain.

At the indoor shooting range, Minor remained in the truck under the shade of a live oak with the windows down. The range was a large rectangular concrete block building with a steel roof. Jamie registered, paid, picked up a target sheet with the outline of a male, nearly as tall as her, put on ear plugs and goggles and walked through the door into the range. This seemed like work all of the sudden. It was dark and damp inside the range. Twenty individual carrels, each about three feet wide, were divided by concrete dividers across the width of the range. The carrel had a shelf to hold the guns and ammo and a shelf to lean on when aiming at the target.

Jamie spotted Junith and walked up to the space next to her. She clipped the 3' x 5' paper target onto the mechanical device and placed a few plastic clothespins to the bottom to weight down the target which was electronically zipped out 25 feet by the press of a button. The length of the shooting range was 300 feet. It was so poorly lit that she could hardly see the target of the shooter at the end carrel who had placed his target all the way at the end of the range.

She stepped next door to watch Junith finish firing her 9 mm clip. Right in the heart of the silhouette on the target, every shot. The acrid fumes from the guns being shot was almost sickening. Junith was 35 years old. Her taunt muscles stretched over her 6-foot structure which was topped with carrot red hair. She had the hazel eyes to go with the hair, but no freckles. Jamie touched Junith's arm to let her know she was there.

They took out their earplugs and screamed to be heard above the gunshots that echoed around the range.

"Hey there. What did you bring with you to shoot?" Junith asked.

"My .38, .45 and 9 mm," she replied.

"Let me shoot your .45. Want to try my 10 mm?"

"Yes!" Her 10 mm was new. It handled so smoothly, especially when compared to Jamie's .38. They traded guns back and forth for about an hour before they packed up everything and headed out to the crossroads.

The crossroads was Brookdale's downtown area and the County seat. On one corner was a small post office, the courthouse and a drug store. On another corner was a cafe called "Joyner's." Across from Joyner's was a fruit and vegetable stand where the locals sold their produce, a Winn Dixie, and the Dora County State Bank. Across from the bank was the Baptist church, a Presbyterian Church and a feed store. There were other minor shops and of course, the county newspaper, *The Dora County Times*. All of Brookdale's stores are on this strip of crossroads. Jamie and Junith parked in front of Joyner's and went in for lunch.

Minor was allowed inside. The owner of the establishment, Agnes, loved dogs. Agnes was born and raised in Brookdale and seldom, if ever left it. Her family had run this establishment at the crossroads for three generations. She was one tough cookie. Agnes carried her overweight torso with a great deal of effort. At 5'5" and 160 pounds, she had a lot to carry. Her short blue-grey hair from a bottle was permed tightly around her large head. Her big brown cow-eyes reflected her keen intellect that was in direct contrast to her slow southern drawl. Her husband, Henry, ran their 250-acre corn farm.

"Good morning, Minor," Agnes said to him as he walked behind the counter and sat down. "How are you doing, big fella? You're as pretty as a show dog. How about some leftovers?"

Junith and Jamie headed to the people side of the counter and were served after the dog.

"We'll have your luncheon special with sweet tea," Jamie told Agnes once she was paid some attention. Her specials were typical of this area. The day's special was fried pork chops, mustard greens, mashed potatoes, biscuits, and apple cobbler. The taste of "home style" cooking was fabulous but it was a real heart stopper with all the cholesterol and fat. Jamie treated herself once in a while to this food and then would diet for a month to even out the effects.

"Do you know anything about that corporation that bought the Livingston property over next to mine?" Jamie asked Agnes.

"Some smart-alec big shot came in here asking me how to get there one day. I asked why he wanted to know. He said he was thinking of buying the property." Agnes always had the poop on the latest happenings. She turned to ring up a customer.

The food was delivered scalding hot. Jamie had to wait for it to cool but Junith jumped right in. "What's the matter? Don't you like your food hot?" Junith asked.

"Not this hot. It burns my mouth," she replied.

"Oh, you are one of those wimps who like warm food. It's bad for you, you know. Lots of live germs grow in lukewarm food," she teased. "Do you remember Joe Koening, the punk who gave us so much grief when we were working at the high school?" Junith asked her.

"How could I forget? It seems as though I spent most of my time taking Joe to your office for something, chewing and spitting tobacco in class, possession of crack, fighting, or skipping. Remember when he spit that junk in my hair?" Before being elected sheriff, Junith had been a School Resource Office at Dora County High School.

"That was your fault," Junith responded. "You never should have let him stand behind you. Anyway, he's a realtor now. He set up the sale of the Livingston property. The land sold for $500 per acre for 5000 acres even though Ray Livingston's son had wanted $2000 an acre. The purpose of the corporation is still a mystery. By the way, how's Fred's mom?"

Mrs. Pellen had suddenly aged quickly. She was 90 years old at the time Fred noticed a drastic change in her ability to take care of herself. At the time, she still lived in the house in which she raised her family. Fred and his sister had hired lots of help to assist their mother. Someone hauled her around town, helped around the house, and prepared meals. But, a decision was finally made and she was moved out of the house. It was traumatic for everyone. Jamie was reconsidering now. The nursing home was so confining. She needed the attention of the nursing home for her body, but she received absolutely no stimulus for her mind.

"Not so good. She's fallen a couple of times. Nothing broken but it's only a matter of time. She refuses to use a walker. Says it slows her down too much," Jamie explained.

"It's hard. I'm going to have to face the same thing in a few years with my mom," Junith said.

"Won't it be easier with your mom rather than with Mark's?" Jamie asked.

"Much. I'll make a decision and put her as close to me as possible and make sure she's well taken care of."

"I thought about Ma Pellen staying at our house," began Jamie.

Junith quickly interrupted her, "Don't do it."

"Why? Hiring a full-time sitter or part-time nurse would be cheaper than a nursing home. Besides, she hates nursing homes," Jamie explained.

"You can't meet her needs without ruining your and Fred's life. I got to go. Want to meet for supper tomorrow night? Mark's working late so it would just be the two of us."

"Come over to my house. I'll cook some hot and spicy Middle Eastern food."

"Okay. About 6:30?" she asked just as her walkie talkie mumbled something in code. Junith jumped up saying someone had been shot at the indoor shooting range. She ran out and took off. The car lights flashed and the siren shrieked.

"Glad I'm not a sheriff," Jamie said to Agnes. She shook her head.

"That indoor range was an accident waiting to happen," she commented.

"Isn't Paul, the guy that owns that place, your nephew?" Jamie asked.

"Yes. I told him that indoors is no place for guns. Too many people in a closed area with deadly weapons. How do you know the people standing next to you know how to handle a gun? I hope he listened when I told him to take out as much insurance as he could afford on the place."

"I heard Hardee's might put up a store across the street beside the Winn Dixie. Have you heard anything about it?" Jamie asked.

"Yeah. Annie Ruth, my first cousin on my mother's side, has bought the franchise. She's got a smart mind for business," she added.

Where did Annie Ruth get enough money to buy a franchise? This town is full of surprises. As if reading her mind, Agnes added, "She was awarded a bunch of money when her husband died. He had lung cancer from smoking cigarettes. A Tallahassee lawyer convinced her to sue the tobacco company. She settled out of court for $1.3 million."

Jamie contemplated suing a company that makes butter when she gets clogged arteries from eating Agnes' food or a coffee company for ruining her teeth and kidneys. The list could be endless. She could get enough to expand her kennel. Maybe she should start smoking. "Won't the competition draw customers away from you?"

"I'm not worried. People said I'd lose customers when the Winn Dixie opened its deli, but I still have more business than I can handle. I had to cut back on running my "all you can eat" specials because I couldn't handle the crowds."

"Do you really make money on those nights?" Jamie couldn't help but ask.

"Oh, my goodness, yes, honey. Like my All You Can Eat Mullet Night I serve coleslaw and French fries instead of a mixed salad and baked potato."

"Is salad that big of an expense item?"

"It's the tomatoes. My price for a flat of tomatoes has doubled in two years."

"Several places in Tallahassee have dropped tomatoes from the salad. I don't really miss it if the salad dressing is good."

"No. A salad has to have tomatoes or it isn't salad. People around here would look at me like I was crazy if I served them a salad without a tomato on it."

That's what makes Brookdale so special: people with old fashioned convictions. Jamie thanked her for a great lunch and called Minor.

While petting Minor and without looking at Jamie, Agnes said, "Junith is right about Fred's ma. Take care of her but not at the expense of your own life. You don't want to ruin what you and Fred have."

"I just don't see how it would interfere," Jamie responded.

Agnes looked at her, sighed heavily, and said, "By the way, Joe Koening has moved his real estate office into the old gas station down by Al Henderson's place. He's usually there if his truck is out front." She didn't miss much. She handed Jamie two big knuckle ham bones for Major and Minor.

"Thanks, again," she said as they left.

Agnes was a special lady. Junith, too. Brookdale had been a good choice for a place to live. It was small and homey without being quaint. It provided an unhasseled feeling. If Jamie could just figure out this land deal next to them, maybe it would help Fred feel "unhasseled" too.

As Minor and Jamie walked out the to truck, she thought that it really didn't bother her what went up next door. But, she knew this land deal really had Fred worried. The privacy of their little 100 acres could be altered if someone messed up that property next door.

At home Jamie exercised on the skier for twenty minutes, ten minutes on the rider and finished off with five minutes on the stepper. Cross training really worked. Her "lonely syndrome" was not overwhelming her, but she did feel like bursting into tears periodically.

The exercise definitely helped. She used to jog five miles a day until the pounding took its toll on her back. Fred still jogged but Jamie used her home gym and alternated it with swimming in the lap pool. It kept her in shape to handle the duties of her kennel. The boys, Major and Minor, anxiously watched her exercise, waiting to take a walk afterwards.

They walked once around the trail before it was time to go to the kennel to feed the canine guests.

4

Fred thought to himself that it felt good to be back in Cairo. His passage through the airport had begun smoothly enough, albeit with a few delays at passport control as people with contacts were taken to the front of the line. He waited thirty-five minutes, standing in a line that seemed to grow longer instead of shorter. Once through passport control, he entered the luggage claim area.

The plane had been crowded and two airbuses had landed within five minutes of each other. The mixture of people from around the globe waited as the carousel droned around and around. After fifteen minutes, there was a unified sinking feeling, however, as no more luggage fell from the mouth of the conveyer belt. Fred had retrieved one of his two bags only to find the other bag had not made it to Cairo. Fifteen other passengers were having the same problem. Fred had been through this before. He quickly crossed the aisle from the carousel to the "Luggage Tracking Company."

"One of my bags did not make it," Fred explained to the quasi-uniformed officer. The Egyptian official was dressed in a freshly pressed brown khaki uniform with a shoulder patch labeled "Luggage Tracking Company" written in English and Arabic.

"Yes, yes. British Air flight?" he asked in broken English with a friendly smile.

"Yes. Here are my luggage claim tickets," Fred offered.

"We need your passport." Fred handed over his passport to the efficient officer who then handed it to someone not in a uniform who promptly walked away with it. Having worked in this area for many years, Fred did not panic. He knew the man would be back. "What color is your luggage?" the officer asked.

"Blue," answered Fred. After several minutes explaining the color, size, shape, combination, and contents of the bag, he was told that someone would take it through customs when it arrived tomorrow and it would be sent to his hotel, *inshallah*, an Arabic phrase meaning "if God wills it."

Fred pulled his solitary bag of luggage through customs and faced the throng of Egyptians waiting for their friends, loved ones, and business acquaintances. A narrow path between the crush of Egyptians gave way, minimally, and Fred made his way to the taxi stand.

Immediately he was besieged by legal and illegal taxi drivers. Several private cars, dilapidated black and white taxis, and luxurious Mercedes lined the roadway.

"Come with me, sir. Good taxi. Right this way," one driver demanded.

"Big car, this way," another offered.

"Cheap price. Follow me," still another yelled trying to gain Fred's attention.

Fred picked a small black and white taxi since he just had his brief case and one suitcase.

"How much to the Hilton?" Fred asked.

"Cheap price. Let's go," the driver said.

"No, first, how much," Fred demanded.

"Fifty pounds," the driver said.

"Too expensive," Fred said, and walked toward the next driver.

"Okay, how much?" the driver questioned Fred as he ran after him and grabbed him by the arm.

"Twenty pounds," Fred offered.

"Thirty pounds," the driver said. "Okay, let's go," the driver grabbed at Fred's suitcase.

"Okay, thirty pounds," Fred agreed. It was the equivalent to about $10. The driver smiled and picked up the suitcase and passed it to another man. By now, there were three men at the taxi: a driver, a luggage loader, and an extra. Fred tipped the luggage loader and got into the taxi. The "extra" asked, "What about me? Where's my baksheesh?" He asked for a tip with such a straight face that Fred had to laugh.

"For what?" Fred asked.

Then, he laughed, too and said, "Masalama."

The taxi, held together by a paper clip and a prayer, raced and rattled down the four-laned super highway to the hotel. The orange haze caused by the desert dust and artificial lighting made it seem as though he was looking at the city through tinted glasses.

Cairo never seemed to sleep. At 12:30 a.m. department stores were still open. Families sat out under the palm trees on the wide grassy median with picnic meals. The laughter could be heard the at stop lights.

The Nile Hilton is the oldest luxury foreign hotel in Cairo complete with floor to ceiling chandeliers, mosaic tile in Islamic designs, and inlaid sculptures of pharaonic times. Fred liked it because of the location and history. It was built in the early 60's and had just begun a restoration that planned to take out some of the very elements that made it elegant. The pharaonic symbols were being replaced, albeit, with new Egyptian artwork which was beautiful depictions of the modern Cairo. Towns, people, and everyday life were portrayed in rich colors on cloth and in wool weavings. The trend was to portray the other Egypt, not just pharaonic Egypt. The solid brass works found on the stairways, lobbies, and hallways were carved with Islamic symbols that served to enhanced the new artwork.

Fred's 12th floor terrazzo floored balcony overlooked the Nile and the Giza pyramids. It was a clear night. The outline of the pyramids could be seen in the distance. The Nile's broad walkway below was crowded at 1:30 am. Lovers were seated on the benches and low walls. Children ran up and down laughing. Men dressed in western garb stood in circles and talked and argued. Fred enjoyed the spectacle for awhile, mesmerized by the action so early in the morning. Finally, he reluctantly returned to his room, slid the glass door shut and thereby shut out the noise and smells of Cairo. He showered, fell into bed and slept soundly until 10:30 the next morning when he heard a knock at the door.

On opening the door, he found an official with his missing suitcase. He tipped the man and phoned in a room service order for coffee. As he sipped his coffee, his eyes scanned his plush hotel room. A feeling of luxury overcame him. He got up, walked out onto the balcony and breathed deeply. Ah, yes. The sounds and the smells of Cairo: the constant blasts of car horns, the gas fumes and the brasso. The brasso smell was particularly strong. The tons of brass artwork in this hotel were cleaned daily. Thus, the brasso fumes were constant. Even opening a window did not help. Fred thought how nice it would be for someone to figure a way to produce odorless brasso. They could make a million.

He ate breakfast in the Osiris Restaurant and watched people come and go as the gardeners watered and pruned the plush garden in the courtyard. As he walked out of the courtyard and down into the Ramses bus station, he spoke to the guards posted at the doorway.

"Where are you going today, sir?" they asked. Fred responded to them in Arabic. It took them a minute to figure out that he had spoken Arabic rather than English. This was the first time he had ever been asked where he was going and when he would be back. The guards told him it was just a precaution and they had his safety in mind. Fred explained he was not new to the area. He also explained that he would be going back and forth to the American University in Cairo and Al Ahram, where the daily newspaper is produced. The guard noted his comments and greeted him good day.

He walked down the steps into the bus depot located just outside the Hilton and was immediately surrounded by taxi drivers. "Need a taxi?" they shouted.

"No, thanks," Fred responded. This area is known as Tahrir Square. At one time there was a walkway around the top of the circular intersection into where no less that ten major roadways emptied.

On his last trip to Cairo, Fred had to walk through open sewage because the workers had hit a sewage line and Tahrir was completely submerged. He carefully worked his way through the throngs of people. Busses sped into the depot, horns blared and little effort was made to brake for pedestrians. Between the loud negotiations among the people who tried to claim one of the few seats available on the busses, and the horns, the bus engines and the gas fumes, it was very uncomfortable and very noisy.

The subway included a walkway underground all the way across Tahrir Square. This made the trip to the university much simpler than the early days of walking across the massive traffic confusion. Fred entered at The Egyptian Museum gate, walked through the main station and came out at the AUC exit, just 100 yards from the main campus of the American University in Cairo. He walked past the main campus to the annex that housed the library and the social sciences. At the gate, a guard at the door checked his briefcase and Fred walked up the steps into the campus.

Work had gone well the first week. A team of very bright Egyptians had been assigned to the project. They generated 1500 questions to be reviewed and refined down to 100 and placed on a final questionnaire. The final product was in the process of being typed and duplicated.

Fred had a meeting with Ahmed at 1:30. He called Jamie at 12:30 from his room using his calling card.

She picked up the phone on the second ring. "Hello."

"Hi, Jamie."

"Fred, how are you? Everything going okay?"

"Yes. We are ahead of schedule, so far. I may be able to finish up a few days early. Guess what?

"What?"

"AUC is moving out by Maadi. The new campus will be out in the desert. Some faculty members have bought land around the university site to build villas. Can you believe it?"

"No. I never thought they'd leave that gorgeous campus downtown," Jamie replied.

"Me either. You taking care of yourself?"

"I'm fine. If you're going to finish early, maybe I shouldn't join you? How early is early?"

"Right now, one week early. It's up to you," Fred replied.

"Well, let's give it a few more days and see. By the way, I got a little news about the Livingston property next door." Fred listened intently while she told him about the cheap sale price.

"Then something's up. I guess it wouldn't do any good to tell you to stay out of it until I got home?"

"Guess not."

"Don't stick your nose too deep into corporate matters. The people who run those places don't like it."

"Yes, dear," she said like a sarcastic obedient wife.

"Okay. I just worry about you, that's all. I'll call you tomorrow. Love you."

"Love you, Baby. Bye."

Fred showered, dressed, and went to the lobby. He found Ahmed at the reception desk.

"Hello, Ahmed. Shall we take a seat in the pub?" Fred ushered Ahmed to the Taverne du Champ de Mars, a cool, quiet Belgium style pub just off the hotel lobby.

Fred had met Ahmed on his first trip to Cairo nearly 12 years ago. They had remained friends and colleagues. Ahmed was a full professor of political science at the American University in Cairo and taught courses at Cairo University, as well. He was part of the educated elite in Cairo. They spent nearly twenty minutes discussing their respective families before Ahmed turned to business matters.

"Fred, I am afraid there is going to be some action taken by the Islamic militants. In an effort to slow down the present government, they are aiming their terrorism not only at tourists, but at businessmen like yourself."

"I've spent many years in Cairo, my friend. I understand the risks. But, terrorism is so sporadic, it cannot be predicted." Fred had completed many studies on the effects of terrorism in Israel and Palestine. It could not be stopped and trying to stop it seemed only to promote it even more.

"In the past yes, it was sporadic. Last night I received word that a group will target major foreign hotels. I suggest you move out of this one and come stay at my home. The Nile Hilton represents foreign businesses and interests. Being the oldest foreign hotel with many American guests, it would be a loud statement if a bomb exploded within its corridors."

"Why don't I just stay at a smaller, locally owned hotel and save you and your family the confusion of me being in your home?" Fred offered.

"No, I insist that you come stay with us. But more importantly, I would suggest you finish your business as quickly as possible and leave Cairo until a calmer time."

Ahmed grew up in Cairo and read innuendoes that Fred, as a foreigner, could not, even though he had spent twenty years studying this area. Fred knew he would never know or understand the city like someone who had been raised in Cairo. Ahmed's insistence that he leave the Hilton must be grounded in some knowledge that Fred didn't have. Fred respected him tremendously. He had to leave with him. Fred went to his room, packed his bags and checked out. He knew he couldn't tell Jamie or she would know something was up and would worry.

5

After talking with Fred, Jamie felt so much better. It really gave her a lift to hear his familiar voice and to know he was safe. She finished cleaning the kennel and exercising the dogs. She had put Major in the exercise pen to get a little sunshine and loaded Minor into the truck. She wanted to find Joe Koening. This was not going to be a pleasant experience. He held a grudge against her for the trouble he got into in high school many years ago. In his mind, she caused him all the trouble.

Joe had done very little in the way of refurbishing the old gas station. He may have painted it, but that is about all. His dented blue Ford Ranger was out front. As Minor and Jamie walked up to the dilapidated door, two male voices in heated conversation could be heard.

"It seems to me it should be worth a little more today than yesterday. I'd say about $5,000 more," said a voice that sounded like Joe.

"Joe, you're playing with dynamite. You won't win on this one. Just drop it," said a voice so low that Jamie couldn't make out who it was, but it sounded familiar.

"This is the biggest deal of my life. I'm not dropping it," replied Joe.

"Just remember, I tried to warn you." There was movement as though someone left. Jamie jerked opened the door and walked in just as the backdoor closed.

There was no a receptionist, just one desk with a wooden chair behind it and two more wooden chairs in front of it. Joe was seated behind the desk.

"Well, if it isn't Mrs. Pellen. Looking for some real estate?" He spoke to her but kept his eyes on Minor whose hair had come up on his back as he growled softly.

"Hello, Joe. No. Just interested in who bought the land next to mine."

"You might want to try the county courthouse. That's where the deeds are filed."

He seemed to enjoy himself. Jamie knew she was not Joe's favorite person, but he was being particularly nasty today.

"I realize that but I was hoping you could tell me a little about the folks and what they will be doing on the land."

"I could tell you a lot of things about a lot of people in this town, but I won't. You'll just have to wait and see."

He had a smirk on his face Jamie would have liked to slap off. Joe stood up and opened the door for them to leave. They left his office and returned home. She would go by the courthouse tomorrow. She had time to take Minor home before picking up Vonnie for lunch.

As Minor and Jamie entered the house, the answering machine was blinking. The first three messages were from clients. She would need to spend part of the afternoon picking up dogs. The last message was from Mary Sue, an old friend from her hometown in central Florida. She wanted to come visit this weekend with her six boys.

Jamie always enjoyed these short visits and tried to schedule them when Fred was not home. He couldn't get used to six kids running around the house. He was an only child, but there were 7 kids in Jamie's family, so the confusion didn't bother her. She dialed Mary Sue's number.

"Hello," some male voice answered.

"Hello. This is Jamie Pellen. Is Mary Sue home?" Jamie inquired.

"Just a minute," he said.

"Hello, Jamie! It's so good to hear your voice. Did you get my message?" Mary Sue said all at once.

"Yes. This weekend would be a perfect time for you and the kids to come up. Fred's out-of-town so we have lots of room," Jamie explained.

"Jamie, I know Fred can't handle us all at once, so sometime Dave and I should come up alone and just visit with you two," she said. "Or, better yet, y'all come down here."

"Trying to get Fred to drive anywhere is impossible. Right now, let's just plan this weekend," Jamie begged.

After fifteen minutes of planning, we decided that she'd arrive Saturday morning and leave on Sunday afternoon. Her husband, a wildlife biologist for the State, was out of town, too. "Let me go, Mary Sue. I need to go see Fred's mom. We're going out to lunch. I'll see you Saturday morning."

The Gardens, the nursing home Vonnie lived in, was located just a few minutes from the Pellen's home. Jamie arrived promptly at 11:00 and found Vonnie dressed in polyester slacks, a polyester print blouse, and white Reeboks. She was sleeping on her bed curled up into the fetal position. Her hair had been permed and her fingernails polished. Although arthritis had mangled her feet, she still prided herself on the fact she could walk unassisted for short distances.

"Good morning. How are you?" Jamie asked pleasantly. She received a blank stare. "Do you have your ears in?" Jamie screamed and pointed to her ears.

"No, I take them out when I'm lying down," Vonnie explained and promptly put her hearing aids in and turned them on. "Say, Jamie, I don't feel like going out today," she said.

"Let's go anyway," Jamie responded. "Come on. We'll use the wheel chair." Jamie opened the wheel chair, placed the eggcrated pad on the chair, set the brakes and pulled open the foot pedals.

"Okay," Vonnie said weakly. She pulled herself up out of bed with a groan, hobbled to the chair, and plopped down with another groan. Jamie rolled her out to the truck. Vonnie pulled her small frame up into the truck and Jamie loaded the wheel chair into the back.

"Joyner's okay for lunch or do you feel like a ride to Tallahassee?" Jamie asked.

"Joyner's," Vonnie replied.

"What's new in the zoo?" Jamie teased.

"Well, last night, I was supposed to have baked pork chops for supper with scalloped potatoes, salad and fresh fruit. Instead I got ground up mush, no potatoes, a bowl of brown lettuce and a cup of canned fruit," she explained.

"What'd you do?" Jamie asked.

"I got up, took my menu to the kitchen to tell them about it. The nutritionist saw me and asked what was the matter. She walked me back to my room, took my tray and menu and brought me a hot pork chop, mashed potatoes and gravy, a bowl of strawberries and a vanilla health shake," Vonnie said with a sound of victory in her voice.

"Good for you!" Jamie said. "It seems they have good food, but it's just not getting to you.

"I've decided to just take it back every time it's wrong. Then they'll learn."

Jamie just hoped they wouldn't poison her or smother her as she slept. Vonnie had confronted the nurses because she had received incorrect dosages of her medicine. She had spoken to the head nurse and sure enough, the hall nurses had not distributed her medicine correctly. At age 95, Vonnie took eight pills three times per day and could tell you the name and description of each one.

"How's your medicine, lately?" Jamie asked.

"Now they bring it in and say, 'You don't have to count. They're all there,' in a snippy voice."

Joyner's was not busy yet. They sat in a corner booth so Vonnie could hear and talked about recent news and sports events, grandkids, and the weather. Lunch, of course, was a typical meal: ham, baked beans, potato salad, rolls, and apple pie. Vonnie ate a fourth of the huge portion and packed up the rest to take home.

"Say, the lady from the library brought me some large print books the other day," Vonnie said.

"Anything good?" Jamie asked.

"They're okay. But, I was going to say she's a different type of bird. She pretends to be sweet and helpful but she's tough as nails. Look at her eyes the next time you see her."

"Why? What happened?" Jamie asked.

"I just asked her where she grew up. She said on a farm up north. I told her I had grown up on a farm up north too, and asked her whereabouts. But, she got very vague, wouldn't tell me what city or even what state. She's hiding something," Vonnie concluded.

Vonnie was glad to be full of good food. She plopped into bed as soon as she got back home. She suddenly looked tired and frail. These lunches exhausted Vonnie but she had to "get out" periodically.

Jamie picked up several canine guests on the way back home and then worked in the kennel. Minor wandered into the woods for a while. He usually stayed gone about a half an hour, chasing deer scents and rabbits. Jamie had discovered that when both Minor and Major were out at the same time, they took off and stayed gone for two or three hours. She worried about alligators, snakes, hunters and other things that went boo in the night. Apparently, as her vet had explained, two dogs constituted a pack, one acted as the leader and one the follower. Once joined as a pack, the dogs' instincts took over and they started to wander, or more precisely, to hunt. They chased the deer and rabbits and eventually returned home, all covered with mud from the swamp and just full of ticks.

Jonathan Lime, the man who managed the Smyth Plantation next door, shoots stray dogs. He said they run the deer to death. It was hard to believe a deer would run down before a dog. He had shot and killed one of Jamie's dogs when they had first moved to Brookdale and before the property had been fenced. She would never forgive him.

The dogs were kept under extreme close supervision now in an effort to prevent these little jaunts, but occasionally she got suckered into believing that they had outgrown the urge to wander. It was similar to Charlie Brown constantly getting talked into letting Lucy hold the football for him to kick but she pulled it away every time just as he let go. You'd think they'd both learn.

When Jamie worked in the kennel, the rest of the world disappeared. She played and talked to the dogs and forgot about everything else. So, when she heard a loud thunderous voice yell "Jamie!" she jumped three feet into the air. She whirled around and saw Junith standing there, hands on her hips, her eyes glaring, and smoke shooting from her nostrils.

"I didn't mean to scare you, but I called your name ten times. What are you doing working in here without the security system on? I could be anybody coming up on you," she lectured.

"I forgot to turn in on. Fred yells at me all the time, too. It's just that I turn it on and then forget to turn it off and I open the door. It screeches at me and then I have to call the alarm company. It just doesn't seem worth it during the day. I always turn it on at night, though," Jamie explained.

"That doesn't make a bit of sense. Most of the violent crime in rural north Florida happens in broad daylight, not the wee hours of the night. There has been a drastic increase in the number of home invasions in this county, too. You are obviously here alone a lot with Fred traipsing all over the world. You need to turn it on," Junith screamed.

"Yes, mam, Sheriff, sir." Jamie knew Junith was right but she always thought the dogs would give her warning. They hadn't barked when she came up, and Minor, the fearless watchdog was in the woods. The runs had been purposely placed so that the kennel faced away from the driveway to limit noise that could be heard from the house. This, in retrospect, had been a mistake because anyone who drove into the driveway could not be seen or heard by the dogs inside the kennel. "What happened at the shooting range? Anything serious?"

"Some woman thought she had shot the complete round in her .22. To make sure, she thought she would look down the barrel and see. The gun went off and shot her in the head. She'll live although I'm not sure someone that stupid should."

"Mary Sue is coming up this Saturday with her brood. Want to come over and swim on Saturday afternoon?" Jamie asked the Sheriff.

"No thanks. Too many children for me. I will see you tomorrow night. Turn on your alarm system."

As Junith walked off, Jamie realized what a good friend she was. She always came by to check on her when Fred was out of town. She's a talented lady who earned a master's degree in English Literature, had traveled throughout Asia and Africa while serving in the military, and had been elected Sheriff of Dora

Country for 2 terms, and was still in the air force reserves. Jamie turned on the alarm system in the kennel and started to work.

On Friday, Jamie delivered several canine guests to their respective homes and went to the crossroads to do her monthly shopping at the Winn Dixie. She also wanted to drop by the courthouse to check on the Livingston land title. Minor was happy to stay in the truck and watch the people in front of the courthouse.

"Hello, Mrs. Pellen. How are you?" One of the clerks at the courthouse was Agnes's niece. There were so many people in Brookdale related to Agnes!

"Well, hi, Stephanie. I'm fine. How are you?" Jamie asked.

"Super. What can I do for you today?"

"I'm looking for the deed to the Livingston property. I want to see who my new neighbors are going to be."

"I can find that for you quickly without even looking up the property number. You are the second one in today to ask that question."

"Really? Who was the other one?"

"I don't know his name but I don't think he is local. In fact, he looked very official. He had on a suit and tie and was tall and gorgeous." They both laughed.

She showed Jamie the deed. It revealed that Healthy Foods Farm, Inc. had bought the land. The deed was signed by the president of the company, Nathan Shoemaker.

She thanked Stephanie and headed for some non-fat-free lunch at Joyner's. She would try to eat healthy next week. Right now, she wanted to read the local mullet wrapper and catch up the latest gossip.

Jamie parked behind Joyner's and left Minor in the truck. It was too busy to take him inside during the lunch hour.

A smile from Agnes greeted Jamie as she sat at the booth in the back of the restaurant.

"What can I get for you, honey?" Agnes called from the cash register.

"I'd like some coffee and today's special," Jamie replied, feeling guilty immediately. The special today was mullet, grits with gravy, tomatoes, biscuits, and cherry pie with a criss-crossed crust like her momma used to make.

To her surprise *The Dora County Times* had a small article in the paper about the Healthy Foods Farm, Inc. It said the company had bought 5000 acres in Dora County. The plans were to begin farming the land immediately and would offer thirty jobs to people in the area. Well, that was positive.

"Jamie?" a familiar voice queried. She looked up.

"Hey, Nancy. How are you?" Nancy was the wife the just retired superintendent of schools who had become a consultant for the State of Florida. He earned three times the salary he had earned at the time of his retirement. She was always so bubbly. She was a petite lady, 5'2", rail thin, had jet-black hair from a bottle, perfect Mary Kay makeup and wore those tight stretchy spandex dresses with fun, flashy jewelry. She had just recently been elected to the County Commission.

"What are you up to?" Nancy asked.

"I just came in for supplies and lunch. How's Martin?"

"He's fine. We just got back from a trip out west where we rode donkeys into the Grand Canyon. While that sounds romantic, it just gets you sore. I found out later that the way to go is in a jeep. How's Fred?"

"He's in Egypt for a few weeks. He'll be back soon. I just read where I'm going to have a new neighbor, the Healthy Foods Farm, Inc. Have you ever heard of them?"

"The company president came to the county commission before buying the land. He agreed the company would pay full taxes and impact fees on the land and provide at least 30 jobs in return for being able to build a business on that land. We have never had a deal like that but it was too good to turn down. We investigated the company records and past history. Our accountant said everything was in order."

"That's good to hear. Have you had lunch?" asked Jamie.

"Yes, I was just on my way out. I've got an appointment. Listen, don't move Fred's mom in with you. You'll be sorry. Trust me. She probably won't want to move in with you anyway. They get very independent living alone for so many years." Without giving Jamie time to respond, she smiled and said, "It was good to see you. Keep in touch."

It struck Jamie that word sure traveled fast in Brookdale. She rolled her eyes to herself and went back to the paper.

Jamie finished her lunch, wrapped a piece of biscuit with butter in her napkin for Minor and walked down the passageway to the back of the restaurant where she had parked the truck. As she turned the corner of the building, Minor was barking wildly at a person walking by the truck. Jamie watched to see what was happening.

The guy had on a baseball cap, light jacket, jeans and Nikes. He went to the front of the truck and tried to open the hood. Jamie yelled, "Hey! What are you doing?" He jumped at the sound of her voice and ran off. She chased after him a short way but lost him as he ran across the highway behind the church. She thought petty crimes like this didn't happen in small towns. Little did Jamie know that she was in for a rude awakening about the crime in small towns.

Jamie went back to her truck, looked under it and in the truck bed to make sure nothing had been damaged. She calmed Minor down, gave him the piece of biscuit and started the engine. Everything seemed to work okay. She didn't know what to think.

She drove across the street to the Winn Dixie and parked right in front by the door, not wanting a repeat of what just happened.

Inside, her basket was loaded up with lamb, hamburger, chicken, sandwich meat, veggies, staples and enough cheese, flour and pizza sauce to make 15 pizzas. The Pellens usually ate pizza 3 times per week. Jamie used a recipe that totals 1200 calories. Fred ate 4 pieces and Jamie ate 2. While it was not fat free, they were proud of the fact that they had cut out the greasy pepperoni.

"Hi, Jamie." She turned to see Penny Meeks, Ashley Meeks' mother. Ashley had been one of Jamie's favorite students.

"Hello, Penny. It's so good to see you. How's the balloon business?" Penny owned several hot air balloons and rented them for rides and sometimes raced them.

Penny was physically what most people would think of a "mother": short hair, practical; not fat but not thin, not muscular but not weak. Just when you thought she fit the stereotype, you found out she piloted balloons.

"It's great. I'm busy every weekend. The folks from Tallahassee keep me booked, especially during Florida State's football season. Except this weekend. I'm going to ride around with just my family. We are going to take three balloons out. Actually, we will be out by you. Why don't you and Fred come along?"

"Fred's in Egypt right now and I've got company coming this weekend, but I'd love to join you," Jamie responded.

"Bring the company along."

"Uh, it's 6 boys and their mother."

She laughed. "That would be fine. Why don't we use your place to take off? We could fly over the national forest and the plantation next to you if the wind is right. I'll call the plantation and make sure it's okay."

"That sounds great. Where do we land?" Jamie asked.

"Wherever the wind takes us. We'll stay up about 2 hours," Penny said.

"What time shall I see you?"

"Let's make it Sunday around 5:30 am." They gave each other a hug and continued shopping.

"Paper or plastic?" the cashier asked as the groceries were unloaded from the basket.

"Plastic will be fine," she replied.

She loaded the groceries into the front of the truck.

The last stop for the day was Johnson's Feed and Seed for dog food. Tommy loaded fifteen bags of generic dog food, ten boxes of pig ears, and a forty pound bag of dog biscuits into the bed of Jamie's truck. "How's your kennel going? he asked.

"Great," replied Jamie.

"Looks like they eat well," he teased. He waved goodbye and flashed a perfectly even tooth grin. Must have had braces, Jamie thought to herself. All the kids these days seem to have perfect teeth. It took away from their personality.

As she drove back home, Jamie began to think about what Nancy had said at the restaurant. "The accountant had okayed everything." Who was the accountant for the County Commission? She called Nancy on the cellular phone. She was not in so Jamie left a message for her to call and leave the name of the accountant.

The alarm system was shouting as Jamie drove up to the house. Her heart pounded through her throat.

First, she let Minor out of the truck. He immediately ran to the back of the house. Then, she leaned over to pull her .38 out of the glove compartment, and eased out of the truck.

Fred would be furious. His warning to leave immediately if the alarm system went off when she came home, rang in her ears. But, Jamie rationalized that it was often a false alarm. If a bird hit a window, or, if a lizard got into the house and crawled across the motion detector beam, the alarm would go off.

As a precaution, she went to the kennel and let Major out. He was going nuts and took off around the back of the house. Both dogs barked and tried to get in the back door. Here was another reason Jamie should have climbed back into the truck. Major seldom got riled up unless someone was around.

As Jamie started toward the back of the house, Junith pulled up in the front yard.

"Get back in you car!" she shouted. She had her 10mm out of the holster and ran to the back of the house.

"Major and Minor are back there," Jamie shouted as Junith turned the corner, as if she couldn't hear their wild barks.

Jamie was torn. She knew Junith could handle the situation and that she would just get in the way and make things worse if there were someone around, but two were usually better than one. Jamie decided to do as Junith had ordered and got back into the truck. The good thing was there were no gun shots.

It seemed like hours had gone by before Junith, Major and Minor came out of the front door. "Turn off your alarm system." The look on her face told Jamie that something was terribly wrong.

She entered the house and hit the four-digit code just inside the front door to disable the system.

"Go back outside. Check your kennel to make sure everything is all right and calm down those dogs. Then go sit in the kitchen," Junith ordered.

"What's wrong. What did you find?" Jamie asked.

"Get the dogs quiet. Then, come back and we'll talk," she said in a very calm voice but her eyes were anxious and deadly.

Everything was fine in the kennel other than a few nervous dogs. It took a while to get everyone calmed down. Jamie gave pig ears to everyone and eventually the noise subsided. While Jamie was in the kennel, an ambulance and another Sheriff's Department car had pulled into the yard. Jamie settled herself in the kitchen until finally, Junith joined her.

"Junith, what has happened?" Jamie begged.

"Joe Koening is in you living room with a bullet through his head."

His being dead was not a concern, for there was no love lost there. But his being dead in her living room made Jamie queasy.

"Where have you been?" Junith asked. Jamie told her about the trip to Joyner's, Winn Dixie, and the courthouse.

"Did you see anyone?" Junith asked.

"Are you accusing me of killing this guy? I have felt like it at times, I'll admit"

"Jamie, just answer my question," Junith commanded.

"Yes. I saw Nancy and of course, Agnes while I was at Joyner's. I saw Penny at the Winn Dixie. I also went by the courthouse and talked to Stephanie Morgan about the Livingston property."

"Okay. Stay in the kitchen until we get finished here."

Jamie did as she was ordered, again. She suddenly felt frustrated. She knew Junith was just doing her job but she didn't like being pushed aside. She brewed some coffee. After what seemed like 2 hours but was probably 30 minutes, Junith came back to the kitchen.

"Well, at least you turned on your alarm system," she said with a slight grin. "Why would Joe be in your house?"

"I talked to him yesterday. I wanted to know about the company that bought the land across the way. He wouldn't tell me anything. He just laughed at me and escorted Minor and me out of his office," Jamie explained.

"It looks as though he was murdered somewhere else and brought to the house and dumped. It must be some kind of warning to you. You must have put your nose where it doesn't belong, again. Who else have you talked to about Healthy Foods Farm, Inc.?"

"You, Nancy, Agnes, Mark, Stephanie and Eddie. Oh, yeah, I mentioned it to Fred on the phone."

She looked at me intently, stood up and said, "Okay. It may be smart to quit asking questions about Healthy Foods Farm, Inc. until we can find out what happened to Joe."

"There's something you are not telling me, Junith," Jamie said determined to find out the truth.

"There's a lot I'm not telling you. The more you know, the more danger you will be in. So stop asking questions. End of conversation."

"Well, there's something else I should tell you. Just before I entered Joe's office, I overheard a strange conversation." Jamie told her what she had heard. Junith listened intently.

"You didn't recognize the other voice?" she asked.

"No, it was too low. I just know it was a male voice."

Junith helped unload the groceries and dog provisions from the truck, stepped outside and watched Jamie turn on the system. "See you tonight," she said as she waved goodbye.

Jamie first sprayed the house down with Lysol. She wasn't sure why, but she just felt she had to. Joe's body had not been there long enough to leave a bad smell but it made her feel better.

Then, she started cooking the couscous, grape leaves, kibbee, sambosa and some baklava. Cooking calmed her down and for a short while, she forgot the events of the afternoon.

The food simmered on the stove as Jamie headed to the pool for a work out. Minor and Major sat beside the pool and watched her swim laps back and forth. It was so quiet. A red-shouldered hawk circled above her as she did the backstroke. After an hour of relaxation and exercise, Jamie was ready to return to work. She went inside to change. The answering machine blinked and beeped at her on her way to the bedroom. She walked over and pressed play.

"Jamie, this is Nancy. The county commission's accountant is Kathy Bennett. You know her from working at the high school.

She is Joe Koening's sister. She married Tommy Bennett. Talk to you later."

Well, isn't that interesting? Jamie wondered if Joe and Kathy are, or were, in cahoots with each other? Would Kathy falsify records to help Joe make an illegal deal?

6

Junith arrived at the Pellen's promptly at 6:30. The smell of turmeric, cumin, hot peppers, and lamb overwhelmed any smell of dead bodies and Lysol by the time she arrived. Junith's mouth watered as soon as she entered the kitchen.

"Um. It sure smells good in here," she said.

They had a glass of wine and sat down to eat. They were both famished, and ate in silence for a few minutes. "This stuff's good. How come you know how to cook so well?"

"Some gals got it, some gals never will. It's not too hot is it? I used jalapeno peppers from the garden. I'm never sure how hot they're going to be."

"No," she said as she wiped her nose. "It sure cleans out the sinuses."

Jamie told Junith about Joe's sister and her connection with the purchase of the property next door.

"That's interesting. Guess I need to go have a chat with her. Is Mary Sue still coming to stay with you tomorrow?" Junith asked.

"Yes. Penny is going to bring the balloons out for the boys to ride. Sure you don't want to come?" Jamie encouraged.

"I'm sure."

"I won't tell her about Joe."

"Good. Don't do anymore snooping, either. Are there rutabagas in the couscous?"

"Yes. They seem to soak up the flavor of the spices so I like them better than potatoes, but there are potatoes in there, too."

Finishing up with 3 pieces of nutty, baklava and a cup of strong mint tea, Junith proclaimed, "Ugh. I'm stuffed," and undid the top button of her jeans.

"Have you heard from Fred today?" she asked.

"Yes. He called this morning. His work is going well."

"You know, I've traveled to a few third world countries and I hated it. The capitals are over populated with dirty, wretchedly poor sick people and the air is so polluted my respiratory system totally shuts down. What is it that you and Fred like so much about Cairo, the epitome of a third world capital?" Junith wanted to know.

"The Egyptians are such gracious and friendly people. It is so drastically different from the US. We find it exciting to visit cultures so different from our own," Jamie responded.

"But why Egypt?" Junith asked in earnest.

"Fred's work is in the Middle East. Cairo is the center of the Middle East, both culturally and politically, and is the hubbub of activity for the whole area."

"Well, it just seems to me that travel within the city has to be hard, pollution is horrific, you get sick from eating bad food or even drinking bottled water. I just don't see why you like to go there."

"Partly because it is *helwa oui* as the Cariennes say, or very nice. We like it. I can't explain it any more than that. Understand, we like Paris, too," Jamie added and laughed because she knew Junith had the same prejudices against Paris as she did third world capitals.

"Well, that figures!" she said.

"Want to play Mortal Combat?" Jamie offered to get to a friendlier topic.

"Oooh. Yes. I haven't played in awhile."

They took turns. Junith was much better at these computer games than Jamie. She found it fun and informative to watch Junith play.

"What's that?" A message flashed at the bottom of the screen what said: *Mind you own business.*

"I don't know but it doesn't have anything to do with that program. Exit out and let's see what's going on." Now it was Jamie who gave the orders to Junith.

She tried but without success to find out the source of the message. It must have somehow been delivered via the Internet after Jamie had signed on this morning. Someone must have automatically downloaded a program with a specific time for delivery after she had signed off. Strange.

"Someone with real computer skills is trying to tell you something," Junith warned.

"But who? I don't know anyone with those kind of skills." They went back to Mortal Combat. It was about 9:00 when Junith left. Jamie checked on the dogs before turning in. Because she felt a little uneasy, she brought Major and Minor inside the house for the night. Since she was being accused of it, she might as well do it. Fred hated dogs in the house. Maybe he would understand about tonight.

7

Fred had moved in with Ahmed on Friday. He and his family lived in a two story villa in Maadi, a suburb of Cairo. It was a beautiful old building with vaulted ceilings, mosaics, and wonderful gardens near the Nile. Maadi is just five miles south of Cairo proper. It is a collection of villas, high rise apartment houses and shanties.

Coffee and sweet rolls were served for breakfast on the terrace overlooking the Nile. "I hear the fundamentalist military training camps have reached as far as your country. They used to be found only in extremists territories," Ahmed said.

"Really? Out west in the barren countryside?" Fred asked.

"I'm not sure. But, I would think they would work better in your sun belt," Ahmed replied.

"Who pays for their training?"

"The fundamentalists are well financed by numerous sources," Ahmed replied. "We'd better get moving to catch the next train."

"Ahmed, I need to call Jamie," Fred said just as they were leaving for Cairo. "What is the best way to get through from Maadi?"

"Come to the university with me. The best way is to use the phones there. Mine may not be completely private so be careful what you discuss. Another option is to see if the American Embassy will let you use their phone, but let's try the university first." They left on the commuter train to Cairo which ended up in the subway at Tahrir Square. They walked to the American University in Cairo. Once in his office, he asked for an overseas line and handed the phone to Fred.

"Dial your ATT connection and the phone number. I'll be back after my class," Ahmed said as he grabbed his brief case and left the room.

The phone rang twice before Jamie picked it up. "Hello."

"Hi, Jay Jay. How's everything?"

"Hey, baby. Not too bad. When will you be coming home?"

"Soon. I need to collect the data for one more set of questionnaires. The interviewers are going out today and tomorrow. If all goes well, I could be home in three or four days." He tried to keep his voice unconcerned and normal, hoping she would not pick up a sign of tenseness.

"Then, I won't try to join you. Your work sure progressed quickly. A month's worth of work in just two weeks," Jamie commented.

"I've had tremendous cooperation and assistance here. The team doesn't get paid until I get the surveys in my hands so they're working double time. What's happening at your end?"

"Not much has happened since I talked to you last," Jamie lied.

"How's my mom?" Fred asked.

"She said she's getting most of her medication now."

"Does she know what she should get for each dosage?" Fred asked.

"I made her a list of her pills and the color she should receive in the morning, at noon and at night. Yesterday, the nurse gave her 5 pills instead of 7. She asked her for the others. The nurse told her that was all she should get."

"She needs all of her pills," Fred said.

"I know. I confronted the head nurse. She met with the other nurses, no doubt to tell them your mother has her smarts and they need to be more careful. Wonder what happens to the ones who don't have their smarts?"

"I'll make an appointment with the administrator when I get home. I'm trying to wrap things up early here. I'll call you tomorrow. I love you."

"I love you. You hang up first," Jamie suggested. This is a game they played. Neither wanted to hang up so they both waited in silence for the other to hang up.

"Okay, I'm going to hang up because I'm calling from the university. Talk to you tomorrow. Bye."

As she put the phone down, she wondered why he was calling from the university? She had hated to say goodbye, but he would be home soon, so no problem.

8

It was around 9:30 when Mary Sue and the kids arrived on Saturday morning. The boys, ages 5, 7, 13, 14, 15 and 17 were just amazing. They were well behaved and they did mind their momma! They hit the pool immediately. Mary Sue and Jamie sat on the porch sipped cappuccino and talked and laughed about the old days.

Jamie and Mary Sue had been best buddies since they were crawling around in diapers. They went through grammar school, high school and Florida State together. They both became teachers even though they had vowed to be anything else but. Mary Sue had quit teaching upon the arrival of her third son.

"It is so good to see you again, Mary Sue. You're doing a great job with the boys," Jamie complimented.

"It's not easy, these days. De Soto City is not the same as when we grew up. Everything is so spread out and unlike our days, everyone does not know everyone. That's why I've decided to home school the two youngest through middle school."

"How do you have the time?" Jamie asked.

"Well, we operate on a tight schedule. I have books from the school and write lesson plans just as if I were in the classroom," Mary Sue explained.

"When do the kids get to interact with other kids their age? That always seems to be the drawback of home schooling."

"They play city league sports and have music lessons. Matt takes gymnastics and Ben is into tennis. They are allowed to play in school sports, too. I mean, we do have to pay taxes even though they are not attending public school. And, the rest of the boys bring home friends so there is plenty of interaction," Mary Sue said.

Jamie had a real problem with home schooling. Most public schools provide textbooks, tests, and in some cases, inservice to the parents who home school their children. In return, the schools received nothing because they could not receive funding for a student not enrolled in the school. Rather than discuss her concerns, Jamie changed the subject.

"Let's eat," Jamie suggested.

After lunch everyone worked in the kennel, and then took out the handguns to target practice for awhile. In the afternoon, they swam some more, played computer games, watched movies, and laughed and laughed. "Mary Sue, do you think the boys would enjoy a trip to a nearby fish camp that houses civil war relics?"

"It might be interesting. How far is it? They have been cooped up in that van for 4 hours."

"About ten miles from here."

"All right, guys, in the van. We have a treat for you!" The boys obediently loaded into the van, no questions asked.

"How do you do it? Why do they mind so well?" Jamie asked in amazement.

"They are under threat of death to behave. They are not always so agreeable, trust me."

They went down to Griffon Fish Camp on the Withlachoochee River. It was around 4 p.m. so it was hot and buggy. They parked out front on the gravel parking lot. The camp consisted of a main building of rustic wood and a tin roof with ten units built just behind it. They were also rustic, but clean and inviting.

They entered the main building en masse. Arnie, the owner, looked surprised at the group until he saw Jamie.

"Hello, Mr. Griffon," Jamie said. "How are you?"

"Well, hello, Mrs. Pellen. I'm just fine. You brought another group to see my relics?" he asked.

"Yes, but this isn't a school group. These are friends from my hometown. Mary Sue Cook, this is Arnie Griffon. He is the owner of the fish camp and collector of all these fascinating bits of history. And these are her sons." The boys nodded in his direction.

"Welcome. How are you boys?" he asked.

"Good," all answered in unison. Jamie wondered what ever happened to fine, thank you and how are you?

"It's a pleasure to have you drop by. Let me show you around." Although Jamie had been on the tour numerous times as a school teacher, she loved to hear Arnie tell about his civil war relics, his collection of perfect arrowheads and his well conditioned whisky still his father had found in nearby woods many years ago. The boys listened and asked questions and of course, wanted to go out and find some arrowheads.

"We've had some heavy rain this week. It might be a good time to look along the shoreline," Arnie advised. "If you find some good ones, I'll buy them from you for $5.00 a piece," he added.

The boys didn't move or say anything but they looked anxiously at their mother. She looked at me and asked, "Do we have time for a short walk?"

"Sure."

Everyone thanked Arnie and left the building. Jamie stopped by the van to pick up her fanny pack with the .38, just in case. A lot of rain may have been good for arrowheads, but it was also good for snakes on the move heading for drier ground.

"Are you allowed to carry that thing around here?" Mary Sue asked nervously.

"I have a concealed weapons permit," Jamie explained.

They followed the well worn trail down to the river's edge and along the banks for about two miles, and turned to backtrack. The boys had a fair collection of mediocre artifacts. "Mom! Come here! Look at this!" yelled Al.

"Wonder what my eldest has found?" Mary Sue said more to herself than to anyone in particular.

Mark was on his hands and knees scraping the dirt away from something. By the time we got to him, it was evident that he had unearthed a human hand. "Stop," Jamie commanded. "Quick, let's go back to the camp and call the sheriff."

The boys ran excitedly back to the camp. The first one back got to call 911. By the time Mary Sue and Jamie arrived, David had called 911 while the rest of the boys had told their story to Arnie. He had given them each a Coke, and had them seated in chairs. The boys showed the pieces they had found around the river bank. Arnie winked at Jamie and Mary Sue as they walked in.

"Look at this one, Mr. Griffon. It's almost a complete arrowhead. It just has one little chip off the side," offered David.

"That looks pretty good, son. I'll give you $3.50 for it."

"Sold!" David exclaimed.

Jamie couldn't believe Arnie had taken the terror out of the afternoon so quickly. They had practically forgotten about the human hand they found and listened intently to Arnie tell stories of days passed.

Junith arrived without the lights. Leaving the boys with Mary Sue and Arnie, Jamie slipped out.

"Over here, Junith." She handed me a shovel as we turned to walk down to the lake. We walked in silence.

"Let's dig around gently to see if it's a whole body or just a body part," she instructed.

"Oh, Junith, yuck!" Jamie exclaimed. Junith ignored her. They dug for five minutes more. It was a whole body. Another Sheriff's car arrived. Deputy Brown ran down to the riverbank and took over Jamie's shovel.

It was a shallow grave. The body was a male. He had been buried face down. Deputy Brown turned the body over. He was a white male about 25 years old, but not someone they knew. Jamie suddenly felt sick.

Junith took one look at her and asked, "You okay?"

"Yes, barely."

"Go back to the camp. The ambulance should be here in a minute. Once they take the body off, I'll be in to talk to you."

Jamie did as she was instructed and was happy to do so this time, but she stopped to empty her stomach on the way. The stench of a dead body in mud overwhelmed her. Arnie looked at her as she entered the camp and handed her a Coke. "Here you go, honey. It will help revive you." Jamie took it greedily and took a big sip.

"What did you find?" Mary Sue asked.

Jamie quietly told her about the body. "The Sheriff will be up in a minute to talk to us all," she added to the group.

"Oh, boy," the boys chorused in excitement. The wait was a brief one. Junith came in just to find out for the record who had found the body. She congratulated Al for his eagle eyes in spotting the body and Arnie awarded him one arrowhead of his choice. They climbed back in the van to go home as Junith stayed behind to talk to Arnie.

The boys swam and played basketball while Mary Sue and Jamie drank lemonade on the porch. "I feel terrible about the boys finding that body, Mary Sue. Will they be all right?"

"Oh, please. It is just one more adventure for them. They don't look any worse for the wear," she comforted.

Everyone went to bed early because they had to get up at the crack of dawn. They ate a huge breakfast, and decided to take a walk before Penny arrived with the balloons.

They walked the trail in the woods and ended up next to the Livingston's land. The road Mark had been working on was cleared and the bed was laid but not yet paved. It looked like someone was already using it, though. There were tracks from what looked like a large truck.

"Gosh. What's going on here?" Mary Sue asked.

Jamie explained what she knew about Healthy Farms Food, Inc.

"You know, you need to watch these people. A company bought the land surrounding the hammock just outside of De Soto City about two years ago. They put in a nice road and said they were going to farm chickens or something like that. They never did. I don't remember why they didn't actually ever build the farm. Now, the land is up for sale."

"Huh. Would you ask around when you get home? Try to find out why they are trying to sell it."

Just as they returned to the house, the balloon entourage turned into the driveway. The front yard was filled with three trucks that pulled trailers with deflated balloons, baskets and fans. Penny had brought her sister, Nancy, brother-in-law, Jimmy and a friend, Maurice to help out. Jimmy and Maurice were also licensed pilots. Burt and Larry, Penny's sons came along to help get the balloons on the way. They, along with Nancy, would be in the chaser cars.

The first balloon was laid on its side. It had stripes of every color of the rainbow. Penny, Burt and Larry ran around making sure everything was set as the pilots readied the basket and helium burners. The baskets were attached, and the fans were made ready to blow up the balloons.

It was a real spectacle. The flattened stripes suddenly became three-dimensional, as the reinforced tear resistant material popped up from the ground. Once inflated, Penny and Burt held the basket while Jimmy jumped in and kept the balloon intact. Al, David, and Steve climbed the small stepladder and fell into the basket, Steve landed head first. Jamie just had to go into the house to get the camera.

The answering machine blinked at Jamie. She started to ignore it but decided to press the play button. It was a somewhat familiar voice saying, "Mind your own business. Stay off the Livingston property." These warnings were getting too routine to be interesting. She quickly hit the save button. She'd play it for Junith later. She hurried out to take a few pictures.

By the time Jamie got back out into the yard, the second balloon was nearly blown up to full size. It was a yellow balloon with a huge green "G" on one side and "Packers" on the other. Mary Sue's husband was a Packer fan. The last balloon was garnet with gold trim and a big FSU on one side and Seminoles on the other. Each basket could hold about 500 pounds, enough for one pilot, and two adult passengers or three children.

Mary Sue and Jamie ungracefully fell from the stepladder into the Seminole balloon, albeit not head first. Matt was lifted into the balloon. He eyes were wide with excitement. Mark and Ben climbed into the Green Bay Packer balloon with Maurice. Nancy, Burt and Larry would follow on the ground with the phone in case anyone needed anything.

The efficiency of the wicker basket was a wonder. All that would be between them and a drop of several hundred feet was a basket. Jimmy had jumped up and down a couple of times before the boys got in. Why? To see if the bottom would hold? Jamie tried to be brave but she had a real fear of flying in that little basket.

Penny picked up her cellular phone, dialed and said, "Hello, Hon. This is Penny. I need a pilot's weather report, please." She wrote down the different speeds of the wind at various levels of altitude and passed it on to Maurice and Jimmy. It was a picture perfect day, not a cloud in the sky and just a mild breeze.

Penny and Burt stepped away from the basket. The burners whooshed and the balloon, basket, and boys quietly drifted away. The kids screamed with delight as the big balloon and basket gently left the ground. Jamie took some great pictures of the boys' faces as they took off. Then Maurice's Packer balloon took off. Just because Mark and Ben were older did not mean they were any less excited.

The hot air balloons lifted so quietly off the ground that Jamie didn't even know she'd left the ground until she noticed the tree tops. Her mind was dwelling on the fact that she was standing in a small basket.

"You okay?" Penny asked.

"Scared to death," Jamie responded. Penny laughed. "How do you direct this thing?" Jamie asked.

"The pilot of balloon is always looking and thinking ahead because the response time of the pump for the hot air is about 5 or 6 minutes. I always have to be anticipating at least 5 minutes ahead," she explained.

"What if you miscalculate?" I asked.

She just smiled at me and told me to relax.

Jamie tried to relax but it was not easy. The quietness of being in the balloon with just the sound of the helium burning up into the huge multi-colored balloon was awesome. They flew over the plantation adjoining our property.

"Look at the herd of white-tailed deer," Penny said quietly as she pointed below. It was so quiet, in contrast to flying in jets which make so much noise, as do the people inside the jets. "Want to pick a pine cone from a tree?" she asked.

"What?" Jamie didn't see how she was going to maneuver the hot air balloon to the exact height to pick pine cones. But, she did. She's good.

"There's blue heron on the lake," Jamie said to Penny. They passed over 5 different lakes each between 3-5 acres in circumference.

They saw a red fox, quail, and winding roads lined with oak trees. The plantation house was a large antebellum style with tall columns and moss laden oak trees surrounding it. "Wow. That house is right out of *Gone with the Wind*," Mary Sue commented. The plantation looked like a fairyland.

"Notice their horse barn and dog kennel," Jamie pointed out as they passed over the largest buildings on the plantation. The horse barn was white with large green shuttered windows. The dog kennel was built in a u-shape with runs built out into a courtyard. The dogs came out to greet them. There must have been fifty adult hound dogs. Three of the runs had puppies who came out to join the fun and barked at the balloon.

Then, they saw a group of 15 small tents and a larger one several miles from the main house. "What's going one? A boy scout camp out?" Mary Sue asked.

"I don't know. It looks more military than boy scout. They have lots of events on the plantation to raise money for charity, like polo and holiday dinners. Maybe they have some function going on," Jamie said.

There was also a small church and several small shanties around it. "Are those shanties for the people who work on the plantation?" Mary Sue asked.

"The Smyth's own the plantation, but Jonathan Lime actually manages the plantation. He wants to move all the workers, mostly poor blacks, off the property or at least to the undesirable edges," explained Jamie.

"So what is he doing?" Mary Sue asked.

"As a house needs repairs, he just doesn't fix it. Eventually, it is condemned and the family has to move out."

"That seems a little cruel. Where do they go?" Penny asked.

"He said it is not his problem," Jamie explained. "I do give him some credit. He does not move the old folks out. Just the younger generation. It's ironic that they raise money for charity the same time they kick people off their land."

"What are those weird looking trees down there?" Mary Sue asked. "I've never seen any like that."

"Which ones?" Penny asked.

"The ones that are greener than the other ones."

Penny laughed. "That's marijuana. It is often grown on the plantations. It is hard for law enforcement to spot it or find it once they get into the plantation. It is grown by the workers and is not usually sold."

"How come you've never reported it?" Jamie asked.

"I would never be allowed to ride over the plantations in this county if I did. Because plantations cover a major portion of the area around Dora County, it would be hard to find a place to balloon."

The two hours went by too quickly. They began their descent over an open field in South Georgia. The ride had been exciting but Jamie was glad to get back on the ground safely.

Penny and her crew loaded up the balloon and basket while Mary Sue and Jamie looked on. In just a short time, everything was packed and loaded, and they were back at Jamie's in no time. The rest of the ballooners had returned earlier and were already swimming.

Jamie said, "How about sandwiches all around?"

Everyone agreed. They all sat out by the pool ate and talked about the exciting balloon ride. The "brood" left around six o'clock. It had been a good weekend, but Jamie was ready for some peace and quiet.

The next two days passed without any more bodies, or gunshots, or warnings. Fred had called each night just before Jamie went to bed. He seemed to be about finished with his work. At least he was safe.

On Wednesday morning, Jamie worked in the kennel for a couple of hours. She was training a Black Lab and a Boxer. The seven month old Lab could retrieve, sit, stay and heel. The Boxer, on the other hand, had a real attitude. The owner brought him in at two years old and asked Jamie to train him. It had been a real test of wills. He would heel and stay, most of the time.

Jamie loaded two of her "guests" to take them home. She turned on the alarm system, put Minor in the truck and took off.

She drove up to Charlotte's place and tooted the horn. Charlotte lived alone on 100 acres at the top of a hill laden with live oak trees overlooking her horse pasture and pond. Her husband had died ten years ago of a heart attack, and while 100 acres is a big responsibility for a 75-year old woman to manage alone, she refused to give it up. Her younger brother had just come to live with her to help out. Charlotte came out of her house looking well rested and relaxed.

"Charlotte, how are you? You look great. Your trip to Atlanta must have done you some good."

"Jamie, Jamie, Jamie," she said so emphatically as she hugged Jamie so hard that she would have laughed but she couldn't breathe. It was as if Charlotte had been looking for her for years and had finally found her. "I had a dream about you just last week," she said as she help Jamie unload the two dogs.

"Are you still keeping your dream diary?" Jamie asked.

"Oh, my yes. My publisher has just finished printing the page proofs and I'm reviewing them before it goes to print. It should be out in time for Christmas."

"I didn't realize you had a publisher for your book. What's the title?"

"*Dream Diaries: How They Help You Get to Know Yourself.* I've kept one for five years. I kept careful records of what I ate, drank, or did out of my routine and the type of dreams I had. I wanted to see what physical and emotional aspects of my life affected my dreams," she explained.

"Sounds fascinating," Jamie had to admit. "I'll be sure to buy a copy when it comes out."

"The publisher will be giving me a signing party in Tallahassee but I insisted on a small one in Brookdale as well. "

"Great! Well, your puppies were fine. I'll see you next time." Jamie stepped into the truck and started the engine.

"Jamie, I wanted to tell you the dream I had about you was not a good one. You were very upset, as if something or someone close to you was hurt. Please be careful," she warned.

"I will," she promised, smiled and waved goodbye. Charlotte was a nice lady but this dream stuff was laid on a bit thick. Now she was using it to predict the future. Jamie wondered how she got a publisher for such nonsense? "What do you think, Minor? Do you think we should worry about Charlotte's dream?" Minor promptly barked and gave her a nip kiss. Jamie interpreted this as a no.

On the way back home, Jamie was behind a milk tanker. It surprised her when it turned off on the road leading into Healthy Foods Farm. In the back of her mind, she heard Junith's warning to keep out of it, but she had to know why that truck turned in there. Rather than follow it as it turned in, she turned in her own driveway. She pocketed her .38, took Minor and Major, and ran to the edge of the property.

Frustrated that she couldn't see a thing from her side of the creek, she jumped across to get a better view of the road. The truck stopped about half way into the property, in the middle of the cleared area, turned around and drove back down toward Highway 20. Maybe he was just lost. He pulled out onto the highway and went back the way he came. Now that was weird.

Jamie and the boys began to walk back home. It had just begun to get dark. It was a gorgeous time of day. Everything turned a kind of dull orange as the sun set and the animals in the woods started to drink and feed. She watched the woodpeckers flit from tree to tree in search of food. The Pellens had spotted three varieties of woodpeckers so far: the Piliated woodpecker, the red-headed woodpecker and the Downey woodpecker. Fred kept a list of the various wildlife spotted on the property. They had 121 different species of birds on the list.

She was so intent on watching and listening to the birds that when a shot rang out, she was disoriented as to which direction it had come. Minor and Major, however, immediately ran off toward the Livingston property. Jamie walked quickly toward her house.

There should not be any hunters on her property. They have posted signs up all around it and it was fenced. That did not really stop anyone from walking onto the property and hunting, however. The plantation did rent their property for hunting for $750 per day per person. The herds of deer were popular with the hunters, but those guns had never sounded as near as this shot.

Maybe someone knew the Livingston property had been sold and figured no one was around to stop them from hunting. At any rate, Jamie felt that the shot sounded too close for comfort. Minor and Major joined Jamie about the time she got back to the house. They were covered head to paw with a stinking mud. She hosed them down, dried them off and took them into the house with her.

Jamie called Junith. She was still a little shaken from the experience. Junith listened and calmly told her it was probably just hunters. "What were you doing over there? You need to stay away from that property. Leave it alone! Someone was trying to tell you something by putting Joe in your house," Junith lectured.

"Okay. But, it's hard not to wonder what is happening. By the way, I saw a milk tanker pull in there today."

"A milk tanker?" she asked.

"That's why I was over there peeking across the creek. I was behind it when it turned in. I wanted to see what it was doing. By the time I got home and walked over there, it was pulling out. On another note, have you identified the body yet?"

"We have a lead but not a positive ID. It looks like it is a drug deal gone bad. Just across the border in Georgia, they are having a hard time keeping drugs under control. He had a bullet hole in the back of his head so he probably crossed someone. The Georgia authorities told us they thought he was traveling with a man in his mid-twenties. Clyde and I are going to look in the river to see if anyone else is buried in the sand or thrown into the river. Georgia is sending a couple of divers, too."

"Sounds like fun."

"Oh, yeah, lots. The last time I went in that river was to search for Gerald Garrison. He had been fishing and did not come home. We found the boat down river about 10 miles but no sign of him. Clyde took one side, I took the other. After five days of searching, we were about to give up. The water is so dark, you can't see so you have to feel your way. I was feeling around and felt something that felt like a body, praying the gators and snakes were somewhere else. I felt the fingers, hand, and arm so I gave a tug and the whole arm came out of the socket."

"Oh, yuck!" Jamie exclaimed.

"Yuck is right. I got out of that water and told Clyde we found him. We went down together and pulled him off the branches that had caught him and prevented him from floating down river. Since that time, this diving for bodies has lost all of its flavor."

"I can see why."

"Listen. Thursday, I'm going to Tallahassee for a meeting. Do you think you can mind your own business for one day?" Junith said almost in a whisper.

"Of course," Jamie said but thought she doubted it.

"Well, try. If you need anything, call Deputy Brown."

"Yes, mam. Have a great meeting," Jamie said as she hung up.

9

At 6 a.m. on Thursday morning, Emily, Jamie's kennel assistant, drove up. She got out of her car with Charlie, her Great Dane. He was a beautiful black haired, muscular built dog with a little white on his chest and white patches on his feet. They headed to the back door. Jamie suddenly realized that she still had the alarm system on "instant stay" so she jumped up before Em opened the door.

"Morning, Emily. Hey, Charlie!" She gave him a good rub and a pig ear and let him sit on the back porch with Minor. "How was your trip?" She had gone out west to see her brother and niece and then to Mexico to sun on the fabulous beaches.

"It was great but it is good to be home. I am tired of hotels and airports."

Emily was twenty-eight years old, had dark hair, big green eyes and a fascinating smile. Her sparkling eyes made you just want to smile back at her. More importantly, she loved dogs. When Jamie had first opened the kennel, she asked Em to be her assistant and Em had quickly agreed.

Em earned a doctorate in statistics with a master's in English from Florida State. She had worked out of her home as an editor for various publishers and as a consultant and statistician for large business firms. To get some "outside" time, she helped Jamie with the kennel. She also had a black belt in Taekwondo, played the piano, and was a natural athlete.

"Help yourself to some breakfast. There is a pan of oat bran muffins and fresh coffee in the pot. I want to finish checking my e-mail before we go out to the kennel," Jamie said.

"Thanks. These muffins look great. What time do you get up, anyway?" Em asked.

"Around 4 am. My body clock is till out of whack from the cruise through Asia and the Middle East last spring. It seemed like every morning we got up, we set our clock ahead 2 hours or back a half an hour or something."

Jamie checked her e-mail on the computer and sent Fred a note. He had his notebook computer with him. Technology was great, but phone calls were still better. One e-mail message was from Jamie's sister in Nevada. She had just moved to a new house. She bought "handyman specials", lived in them until they were fixed up enough to sell for a profit, and then move again. She made her fortune this way, but it seemed like she would get tired of moving.

There was also a note from Mary Sue. She said the property bought to set up a chicken farm had a road put in and was left empty for about six months and then put up for sale. No one had any information about why the deal had fallen through but she was still looking into it.

The next e-mail was from someone's address Jamie did not recognize. Normally, she just skipped the unfamiliar mail. For some reason, she decided to opened this one and read it. Her face must have shown her dismay. Em said, "What's wrong, Jamie?"

"Oh, nothing. You know how people abuse e-mail on the computer." She did not want Em to see this message. The message said:

You need to quit asking questions about your neighbors. Curiosity killed the cat and can kill you. Mind you own business.

Jamie printed it out so she could show it to Junith on Sunday once she returned. The e-mail address is a public one so anyone could have sent the message. She turned off the computer and poured herself a cup of coffee.

"Now, what are you doing?" Em asked, her mouth full of muffin.

"I want to put some bread on for lunch," Jamie responded.

She put some water, prepackaged dough mix, and a little packet of yeast, and a half cup of oat bran into the bread machine. "That sure looks easy," Em commented.

"It is. Before bread machines, I seldom made homemade bread. When I first bought my machine, I carefully measured the water, salt, flour, butter, dried milk, sugar and yeast. I hardly ever got the exact measurements so my bread never came out quite right. Now, all I have to do is dump a box of bread mix in the machine and voila! Wonderful homemade bread. Ready to get started?" she asked.

"Ready," Em said.

After turning on the alarm system in the house, Em, Jamie, and the boys walked out to the kennel. They stopped dead in their tracks when they reached the kennel door. On the door was painted a message that read "Mind your own business" written in John Deer green.

Em and Jamie looked at each other. Jamie had not heard a thing last night, but this was not on the door when she checked the kennel before going to bed.

"What does it mean?" Em asked.

"Guess I'd better bring you up to date on what's happened since you were gone. Let's talk while we clean up the kennel."

Jamie filled her in on all of the events so far, except for the e-mail.

"Why don't I come out and stay with you until Fred gets back. Two are always better than one," she offered.

"I can't say that I don't want the company, but I would just worry about you getting hurt."

"Too bad. We'll finish up here and I'll go home and get a few things."

"Thanks, Em." Jamie gave her a big hug.

The phone rang in the kennel. It was Fred. Trying to control the strain in her voice, Jamie took a deep breath and said, "Hi, baby."

"What's wrong? You sound upset." He could always tell her feelings by her voice. She debated whether or not to tell him everything.

"Em is back. She's here helping me now. She's going to stay with me until you get back. When do you think that will be?"

"Today if you don't tell me what you're hiding from me. I just got your email, but you seem to have left out a few details."

"Fred, there's so much."

"Stop beating around the bush." She told him about the gun shot, Joe's body, about the e-mail, the dead man buried on the river bank, and about the message on the kennel.

"Have you told Junith this information?" he asked.

"I was going to call Junith but she is at a meeting today. I'll tell her tomorrow or if she calls tonight."

"Then call Clyde Brown. This is getting serious. I need two more days here and then I'll be home. They can mail me the questionnaires and you can input the data for me. Call Clyde." He hung up.

Jamie did as he suggested. "Deputy Clyde" as she called him came right away.

Clyde Brown was 6'3", muscular build, black, and spoke in a Midwestern accent. He was always quiet, pensive and methodical. Nothing seemed to rile him. He was originally from Milwaukee. His family had moved to Brookdale when he was in middle school. He graduated from the police academy in Atlanta three years ago and received many job offers upon graduation. He chose to return to Brookdale to raise his kids and to be with his dad. He and his extended family also own a peanut farm in north Dora County.

He listened to Jamie's story, took a copy of the e-mail and a picture of the message on the kennel door.

"Walk me over to where you heard the shot."

The three of them walked over toward the creek.

"Stay here a minute," Clyde said as he jumped the creek and walked up and down the semi-finished road. He stopped, picked up something with a handkerchief, placed it in a plastic bag and came back.

"Well, here is the shell from a 12 gauge. Another item almost impossible to trace." Clyde looked concerned. "Jamie, you have stepped on someone's toes. I don't know what you did, but you need to lay low."

"I hardly even asked any questions. I'm not sure what it is I'm doing to get someone so upset."

"I'm going to try to trace the e-mail warning, but it will be difficult. That paint on your kennel door is too common to even try to trace. Stay away from the Livingston property and the property line. The shot you heard may have been a hunter but you may have been the hunted. I don't think they were trying to shoot you, not with a 12 gauge. But, I do think they were trying to scare you."

After Clyde left, Em and Jamie went back to finish the work in the kennel. They hosed down the inside, and fed and watered the dogs. They finished up around noon and went inside for lunch, taking Charlie, Minor and Major with them.

Just as they got in the back door, the boys took off toward the front of the house. Em and Jamie followed the dogs around front to find Eddie and Tammie in the driveway. They called the dogs back.

"Hi, Jamie. Hi, Emily," Eddie greeted us as he got out of his truck. "Just dropped by to make sure everything is okay." Tammie waved from the truck but did not get out.

"Everything is great. Fred will be home at the end of this week," Jamie offered.

"That's a little early isn't it?" Eddie asked.

"Yes, but he found he doesn't need to sit over there and punch in data. He figures he can bring it home and I can punch it in," she said with a grin.

"Sounds like a good idea," he said laughing. "Well, call if you need anything. One of us is home most of the time."

"Thanks, Eddie." Eddie got back in his truck and waved as he drove down the driveway.

"Did you see the gun he had in his truck?" Em asked.

"Yes, Em, but I don't think we need to worry about Eddie." Like most people in rural north Florida, Eddie had a gun rack and a shotgun in his truck. It was a 12 gauge. But, then, that was the same type of gun most Brookdale folks carry in their trucks.

As they turned to go back to the house, a car pulled into the driveway and the horn blew. It was Diana Johnston, a lifetime resident of Brookdale. She knew everything about everyone, and then some.

"Hello, Jamie. Emily," she yelled from her car as she got out to unload her Rottweiler, Sebastian. They walked over to her car.

"Do you have room for my puppy for a few days? I'm going to St. George Island and he positively hates it there."

"Sure. Just two days?" Jamie asked.

"I'll be back and pick him up on Sunday, if that's okay?"

"Sounds great." Emily took Sebastian to the kennel. "He's not losing any weight, Diana," Jamie teased.

"He's on 20 mg. of prednisone for his arthritis. It makes him bloated and ravenous. He nearly takes my hand off when I feed him," she explained.

"Leave him with me for a month. I'll get the weight off, wean him off prednisone, put him on rimidyl and he'll be a new puppy," she offered.

"Oh, I couldn't be without him for two weeks. I tried rimidyl. I even got him off the prednisone. But the rimidyl didn't work. He couldn't get up, poor thing. Broke my heart. So, I put him back on the prednisone."

"I'm going to call your vet and find out what happened. I have never heard of rimidyl not working," Em said.

"Go ahead. When I get back, we'll make a plan to get the weight off. I know I need help with him." She turned her attention to the truck she had passed on the way into the driveway. "Was that Eddie and Tammie leaving as I drove up?"

"Yes. He was just making a neighborly call. Fred's in Egypt," Jamie informed her.

"It's good to see Eddie come to life again. We went to high school together. He was a real lady's man. He drank gallons even back then, so it's no wonder he became an alcoholic later in life."

"That's too bad." Diana knew so much about everyone that Jamie preferred to listen to her rather than talk.

"Yes, it is. His first wife was a darling lady. Put up with his nonsense too long for anybody's good. He met Tammie and she clung right to him. She seems to have some power over him. Some women can do that to some men, making them act like they are under some kind of spell. He would do anything for her. It's almost scary."

"Well, they both seem happy enough. She's got a good job and Eddie's got several odd jobs going," Jamie added in a positive note.

"Yes, but you know, I don't think an alcoholic ever fully recovers. They are in constant fear of succumbing to the temptation. Well, let me go. See you Sunday."

Jamie waved goodbye just as Em emerged from the kennel. "Hungry?" Jamie asked.

"Always," Em responded.

The smell of baking bread overwhelmed them as they entered the kitchen. Jamie laid out some Stilton cheese, bananas and dates for lunch along with the fresh bread.

As they ate, they talked about the business, Em's trip, Fred's trip, anything but warnings, guns, or murders. When they finished and cleaned up, Em said, "Jamie, I'm going to run home to get my computer, a few clothes, and a manuscript I'm working on. Do you have any pick ups or deliveries I can do on the way?"

"No. Everyone is taken care of right now. When will I see you?" I asked.

"Let's see. It's 1:15 now. I should be back by 4 p.m. If I run late, I'll call you."

10

After Em had left, Jamie decided to use the time to exercise. She was really uptight so she stretched her muscles extra before she mounted the skier. She skied for thirty minutes and then walked out to the pool. The blue sky was reflected in the pool and a slight breeze blew against her face. Jamie decided to swim a little. The sun was warm but the water temperature had dropped from 89 to 83 degrees, which was a little chilly by her standards.

Fred had suggested a gas heater for the pool when they moved in. It cost about one dollar per degree to heat the water, but it was money well spent. They had tried in vain to get a solar heater but, at that time, no one in North Florida seemed to be interested in installing one. Jamie reminded herself to check the temperature in the mornings so she could turn on the heater if the water was too chilly.

After her laps, she played "excite the dogs" with the boys. Jamie threw a ball at Major's snout. The ball would bounced off his nose and splashed back into the water. The boys barked and drooled all over the place.

After all this excitement, she made both boys jump in for a brief swim. One last go round with the ball and then she let Major have the ball. He promptly popped it and carried it into the bushes where he guarded it for a while.

She dried off and then toweled the boys off. The phone rang, so she ran into the house and turned on the system before answering the phone.

"Hello," she said.

"Hi Jamie. It's Mary Sue."

"Hi. Did you get home okay?"

"Oh yes. I just wanted to thank you for such a great time. The clan is ready to go back up there. I told them we had to give you at least a 6 months recovery time," Mary Sue teased.

"I really had a super time, too. You have a bunch of neat kids. Any repercussions from finding a body?" Jamie asked.

"Not at all. They think they're big shots. The story gets bigger every time it's told. But I called to tell you what Al and David told me about their balloon ride."

"What's that?" I asked cautiously.

"Two things. First, just as they took off from your front pasture, they passed over the land next door to you—not the plantation but the other side, where that farm is going to be. They noticed a bunch of dead trees on the back side of the property, near where the end of the road is going to be."

"Really? Well, you know about five years ago we had a hurricane come through Brookdale. It spun off numerous tornadoes which knocked down most of the water oaks. These big, beautiful trees have a very shallow root system. A strong wind just topples them," Jamie explained.

"That could be it but it reminded me of the hammock land with the dead trees. I just wondered if there was some connection?"

"What was the second thing?" I asked.

"This may be nothing and the boys were a little disoriented as to where they were when they saw it but there was a man dressed in soldier gear holding what they thought was a shotgun."

"How long had they been airborne when they saw him?"

"It was at the very beginning of the flight. They were so excited, as was I, that they forgot about it until we were talking about the balloon ride on our way home. The interesting thing was that when the man saw the balloon, he ran under an oak tree so you could not see him. Had he not done that, they probably would not have thought twice about it."

"Thanks for letting me know. You do not have to wait six months to come back, you know. I really enjoyed seeing you."

"Thanks! I'll talk to you again soon. Bye bye."

Jamie and Mary Sue had gone their different ways since college but they are still just as close as they were when growing up together as best friends.

The phone rang again as soon as she had put it down.

"Hello."

"Hi, Jamie. This is Amy Lou. Could I drop Buttons by for a couple of days?"

"Sure. I've got plenty of room," Jamie said.

"Okay. I'll be by in about a half an hour. If you're not there, I'll just put her in the pen."

"I'll be here. I'm working on the accounts."

"Fine. I'll see you soon."

Jamie settled down to play accountant. She needed to update her kennel accounts. She pulled out all the receipts for dog food, dip and shampoo, utilities, and payment from boarding fees. She had invested in a database program which she used to itemize all expenditures, to keep track of her customers, and to keep records of the dogs and their needs so repeat customers were not continuously bothered about medicines, and other routine information. She made a note to call Diana's vet.

The kennel made a good profit. Fred had thought it would never work. Jamie's formula was simple: She did for other people's pets what she wanted done for hers. The kennel was filled to three-fourths capacity for eight months of the year. Two months, June and July, it was filled 100% but in August and September, she did well to have the kennel one-fourth full.

Jamie looked out the window to see Amy Lou get out of the car with her Shitzu, Buttons. She turned off the alarm and walked out to greet her. Amy Lou carried Buttons while Jamie carried her blanket, a child size recliner, and a few dog toys to the kennel. Amy Lou carefully placed everything in the run. Buttons thought this was her second home. She jumped up in the chair and settled in.

"Jamie, your kennel is just great," Amy Lou said. "You know the other kennel owners are really upset about the success of your business. You are a little more expensive but the services you offer are well worth it."

"Thanks, Amy Lou. I try to treat your pet like I treat my own," Jamie responded.

"Well, it shows. I wouldn't leave Buttons anywhere else but with you. By the way, you sure have a way of tripping over bodies. My sister lives in Georgia. She said the last body you found is from her hometown, Mayetteville, in south Georgia. His mother lost control of him early on. He's been a drug dealer for five years and he was only twenty."

"Really?" Jamie asked.

"Yes. He was a mess in middle school. His mother did everything in her power to straighten him out, but the streets got hold of him and she never got him back."

"That is really sad."

"Yes, it is. Well, let me go. I'll see you in four days." She got back in her car as she explained she was going to New York City for a long weekend for some culture and exotic food.

Jamie entered data for another half an hour before she finished with the last receipt. She called Diana's vet in Tallahassee. "Hello. This is Jamie Pellen. Could I speak to Dr. Hamilton, if he's available?"

"Dr. Hamilton is with a patient. May I help you?" the receptionist said.

"I'm calling about Diana Johnston's Rottweiler. He's presently staying at my kennel in Brookdale. She left me 20 mg. of prednisone for his arthritis and she told me she had tried rimidyl but it didn't work. I just wondered what dosage the rimidyl was?" Jamie asked.

"We don't talk to third parties about our client's pets," she said coldly.

"Then, let me talk with Dr. Hamilton. I'll hold until he is free," Jamie said in her sweetest voice. After fifteen minutes, Dr. Hamilton came on the line. Jamie was sure the receptionist had already explained what she wanted but he acted like he didn't know. So, Jamie patiently explained the situation.

In a cold, calm voice, Dr. Hamilton said, "We don't talk to third parties about our client's pets. If Ms. Johnston wants to know the dosage, she can call us."

Jamie took a deep breath. It would do no good to get angry. "I'm just trying to help her. I have never heard of rimidyl not working. Her dog is 50 pounds overweight, bloated like a balloon, and I'm sure the prednisone is not helping that any. He's going to die shortly if this pattern continues. Every time I see him, he's bigger and bigger. I just thought you would want to help."

"The rimidyl dosage was 100 mg," he blurted and hung up.

Well, that explains it. The dog weighs 150 pounds. He is supposed to take 1 mg. of rimidyl for each pound so he should have been taking 150 mg twice per day. He was severely under dosed. No wonder it didn't work. Jamie would need to work on Diana's feeding patterns and get her to wean Sebastian off prednisone and start taking rimidyl.

She heard Em drive up. She shut off her computer and went to the door to meet her. Jamie opened the door at the same instant she realized that the security system had not been turned off.

"*You have violated a protected area. The police have been called. Leave immediately*," bellowed from the loud speakers as bells and whistles screeched. The dogs barked wildly and Em covered her ears.

Jamie turned off the system and waited for the alarm company to call. The system automatically disconnected the phone line to put the call through to the company.

The phone rang. "Hello, I set my system off. Sorry."

"No problem. Could I just get you code number?"

"13324."

"Okay. Thanks. Bye."

"Sorry, Em. I forgot I had turned it on. You see why I leave it off sometimes?"

"Yes, but it is a small inconvenience to pay for the warning it provides." She was beginning to sound like Junith. They unloaded Em's car.

"Want to take a walk before supper?" Jamie asked.

"Sure. Let me just put on my walking shoes," Em replied.

They locked up and took the dogs with them. Jamie carried the .38 in her fanny pack, just in case.

It was a very hot afternoon for late September. Usually the weather broke after the heat of August passed. Sweat rolled down their necks as they sauntered down the trail. They laughed and talked while the dogs ran off into the woods to scare up quail and deer. They enjoyed the walk so much that they decided to walked the circuit again.

Before Jamie and Em returned to the house, they exercised the dogs in the kennel and filled up the water bowls. One day she would invest in the automatic watering bowls, Jamie thought as she filled the galvanized water buckets. It was 7:00 before the kennel was closed for the night.

11

The boys were left on the porch with one ham hock each. "What do you want for supper?" Jamie asked Em.

"I brought some hot wings and a couple of salads from the store. I didn't want you to cook and I didn't want to either."

"Ooh. Thanks. I love wings." My poor arteries, Jamie thought. She had eaten at Joyner's twice in one week, stilton for lunch and now wings.

They decided to eat watching the news. Fred and Jamie had bought a DSS, small satellite dish when they moved to Brookdale. Now, instead of three stations of programs not worth watching, they had access to three hundred useless programs. The redeeming virtue of the extra programming was access to international news. The German Journal has the best coverage of overall world events.

They caught the end of a story about a hotel being blown up. Jamie quickly turned to CNN Headline News. They were just beginning the story. The Nile Hilton in Cairo, Egypt had been blown up. They were still digging out survivors from the rubble. Muslim militants were taking the credit for the blast.

Jamie almost choked on a wing. She slammed her plate down on the coffee table and ran to the computer to see if Fred had sent and email about the blast, hopefully saying he was okay. Tears started to form in her eyes. Em placed her hands on Jamie's shoulders.

"He's okay, Jamie. Fred can take care of himself. He's okay."

Jamie frantically signed onto the Internet, trying to see the screen through her tears.

"There is an e-mail from Fred!" she screamed. They both read it as soon as it came on the screen.

I moved away from the Nile Hilton 2 days ago in anticipation of the bombing at the hotel. I did not tell you because I did not want you to worry. Due to the bombing, I plan to leave Cairo today and will be home by Sunday. I will stop overnight in Paris to buy some books. The phone lines are overwhelmed with news coverage use, so I cannot call you from here. The American Embassy folks let me use their computer for this e-mail. When I arrive in Paris on Saturday, I will call you. I will be fine. All my love. Fred

After reading the message, Jamie started bawling. Em told her it would be okay, that he was fine. Finally, she stopped crying and apologized. The phone rang just as Jamie was washing her face. It was Junith.

"Have you heard from Fred?" she asked

Jamie told her about CNN's report on the bombing and Fred's e-mail.

"Fred can take care of himself. You know that so stop worrying. He will be home before you know it. Is Em still with you?" she asked.

"Yes. She's staying until Fred gets back. Are you back from Tallahassee?" Jamie asked.

"No. I'll see you tomorrow," she said and then hung up.

"That Junith, I tell you what. She doesn't miss much," Jamie commented more to myself than to Em.

Needless to say, Jamie had lost interest in eating. Em finished up the wings and cleaned up the kitchen while Jamie put some water down for Charlie, Minor and Major. They would sleep indoors tonight. She made sure the security system was turned on, took Minor in her room, and then went to bed to read herself to sleep. Major stayed in the kitchen. Em set up her computer in the living room and worked until around midnight, turned off the lights and then took Charlie in her bedroom.

Jamie was suddenly awakened by Minor's growling at her bedroom window. She looked at the clock. It was 2:30 am. Jamie jumped up, grabbed the 12 gauge and did what she was always told not to do: she peeked out the window.

The area around the house and kennel was well lighted. There were halogen lights on each corner of the house and kennel. The lights went on automatically at dusk and off at dawn. Unfortunately, the light on her bedroom side that overlooked the back of the kennel had apparently burned out. It was pitch black. Minor continued to growl.

Jamie quietly stepped out of her bedroom to try a different window. It was strange that Minor growled and didn't bark. He usually growled at things or people he knew but didn't like. He would bark at something new. Major was at her bedroom door when she opened it and walked to the living room window to peek out of the mini-blinds. This area was well-lighted. There was not anything out of the ordinary.

Jamie petted the boys and started back to her bedroom. At that instant, the dogs ran head of her, jumped over the bed and barked ferociously at the window. Now she was scared.

Em came out of her room, saw Jamie with the shotgun and whispered, "What is it?"

"I don't know. It could be a wild animal." Charlie joined the frenzy at the window. Em and Jamie allowed them to bark, and tried to decide whether or not to let them out to go after whatever was out there.

"I'm going to call Clyde. Something's out there," Jamie said trying to be brave.

She picked up the phone. "There's no dial tone," she said in a whisper.

"Here. I brought my cellular phone in from the car. Use it." Thank God for small favors.

"Clyde, this is Jamie. Someone or something is prowling outside my house."

"I'll be right there. Don't open the door or go outside."

"He said to he'll be right here and not to go outside," Jamie relayed to Em. "Let's find a good corner behind something and away from the windows. You take my 9 mm and I'll keep the 12 gauge."

They decided to go in the dining room and turn over the table and hide behind it. That way they could jump out of the window if they got cornered. The dogs barked like crazy at the bedroom window.

"Em, I'm going to have to go peek out of that window."

"Stay away from the windows. Clyde should be here any minute."

"I'm not going outside. I have to look and see if I can figure out what they are barking at." Carefully, she eased over to the bedroom window and pulled up one mini-blind at the bottom of the blinds. At that instant, the kennel's security system went off. She ran to the kitchen door to go out.

"Stay inside, Jamie. Stay inside!" Em yelled.

They both looked out of the kitchen window. About one minute went by when they noticed a spark of light in the kennel. "Look, it's growing bigger," Em said.

"It's a fire!" Jamie screamed as she ran to the kitchen, grabbed the two fire extinguishers kept there. "Follow me and keep me covered in case someone is still out there."

As she ripped opened the kitchen door, the house security system went off. “Oh, help,” she groaned, and let it scream. Now both systems blared warnings. The noise deafened them as they ran across the yard to the kennel.

The fire had not spread very far but it was intense. It had been started at the empty end of the kennel near the food and supplies. Jamie sprayed the fire as Em got the dogs out into the exercise pen. The damage appeared to be minimal, a months supply of dog food was ruined and the walls were charred, but Jamie was afraid to think of what the damage would have been if Minor hadn’t woken her up.

Clyde drove up just as they had shut off the security system’s squawking.

“Why are you outside? What happened?” he yelled as he jumped out of his car and rushed over to them.

Jamie explained about the dogs frantic barking, the dead phone, the alarm system going off and then spotting the kennel fire. He called the fire department to come out and look at the damage and the cause of the fire.

Brookdale only has a small volunteer fire department. Jamie hated to wake up Wally and Bubba at 3 a.m. but Clyde insisted that they needed to look at the damage as soon as possible to determine the cause, as well as for insurance purposes.

Clyde also called for some backup to look around to try to trace footsteps and vehicles tracks. The fire truck pulled in just ten minutes after being called. The Sheriff Department’s backup team arrived five minutes later. Junith was the back up team.

“So, you are back?” Jamie asked. She just glared at me.

She didn’t look pleased to come out at this time of morning. Em and Jamie left them to do their work. They made some strong coffee, muffins, and sandwiches.

Everyone came inside around 3:30 am. Bubba said the fire had been deliberately set with a bit of kindling and some dog food. It would have taken a lot more than that to spread across the whole kennel but could have caused smoke damage. The smoke would have had a definite affect on the dogs.

"You might want to think about putting in a sprinkler system in the kennel. It wouldn't cost that much but could save those dogs if a strong fire started." Bubba's suggestion was well founded. Jamie would talk to Eddie about it the next time she saw him.

Clyde and Junith reported that there was one set of footprints around the house and over to the kennel. He traced the steps over to the woods on the Livingston property side but lost them once in the woods.

"What happened to the light over by the kennel?" Junith asked.

"I didn't notice that it was burned out until tonight," Jamie answered.

"That might be because it isn't burned out. It is just out. There is no bulb in it. Did you just forget to put one in?" Junith did not have a great deal of patience when she was in a good mood. Her questioning methods in the wee hours of the morning left a lot to be desired.

"No, Junith. I have a carton of the bulbs I always keep on hand. When one is out, I change it immediately. Our phone was dead, too," she added.

"Yes, the telephone wires to your house have been cut. You need to call the phone company to have it fixed," she informed Jamie.

"By the way, have you heard anything new about the body we dug up?" I asked.

"Yeah. He was from Georgia. We turned the body over to the state troopers. It's out of our hands."

They found they were all suddenly very hungry. They ate ham and cheese sandwiches, muffins and drank dark, black coffee as they theorized about who would have set a fire in the kennel. They did not come up with many answers, just a plethora of questions. When everyone had gone, Em went back to bed, but Jamie couldn't sleep so she cleaned up the mess in the kitchen and went to look over the kennel.

12

Jamie looked around her kennel. One wall would have to painted where fire had stained the wood. The smell was still pretty strong so she left the dogs in the exercise pen, opened all the doors, and turned on the large attic fan full blast. Jamie first got out a halogen bulb and replaced the missing one. After hosing down the dogs and the kennel, she gave all the dogs a good rub and talking to so they were not afraid and put them back in their own run. Once fed and watered, they settled down.

The phone in the kennel worked so she called the phone company. They promised to be out first thing to fix the lines.

Back at the house, Em was up and about. She had made more coffee and was working at her computer. Charlie greeted Jamie at the door.

"Em, thanks for being here last night. I would have freaked without you."

"You freaked with me, Jamie. But, you're welcomed. Hopefully tonight will be a bit more peaceful."

"What are you working on so hard?" Jamie asked.

"This evaluation report published for Florida Pharmaceuticals. I completed the evaluation but something's not right about this published report. I cannot put my hand on it. I think they may have altered the numbers to make themselves look better before publishing the report. Of course, I'm the only one outside of the company who would notice."

"Doesn't my quasi neighbor, Jonathan Lime have something to do with that company?" Jamie asked.

"He sure does. He is one of the partners," Em said as she frowned and stared at her computer screen.

Jamie left her alone so she could get some work done. She changed to swim laps. Minor and Major sat by the pool and watched her. Swimming allowed the mind to wander freely once a rhythm was established. Her mind flipped around the events of last night from worrying about Fred, to trying to figure out who had taken the bulb out of the floodlight, to why anyone would try to burn up the kennel. By the end of her swim, she was worn out physically and mentally.

She laid out in the chaise in the sun just long enough to warm up and dry off. "Jamie, telephone," Em called from the house.

"Ugh, boys. We'll take a walk after I change," she explained to Major and Minor. The three of them walked into the house.

"Hello," she said in her best business voice.

"Hi, Mrs. Pellen. This is Frank McNabb. How are you?"

"Fine. What can I do for you?" Jamie asked. They was a slight hesitation on his part.

"I wanted to board my dog for about two weeks. Do you have space for him?"

"Starting today for two weeks. Yes, I do have room. What is his name?"

"Thor."

"Shall I pick him up or will you be bringing him out?" she asked.

"I'll bring everything and label it in case you are not there when I arrive. I also have some treats for him."

"Someone should be here. If not, just put him in the exercise pen and hang the bag on the door."

Since this was his first stay, she tried to get all of the medical information, vet's name, and information about Mr. McNabb for the computer file. When she hung up, she called Thor's vet and asked them to fax his proof of kennel cough shots and vaccinations.

She was so tired but wanted to walk the boys before trying to nap. "Em, I'm going to take the boys for a walk. Want to come?"

"No, I need to get this worked out. I'll take care of the kennel this afternoon for you. You just relax some."

"Thanks."

The woods seemed loud. The birds chirped, the squirrels ran around, and the breeze blew through the trees rustling the leaves and caused the pine trees to sway rhythmically. The maple leaves had just begun to turn red. The leaves on the popcorn trees had turned red on one side and yellow on the other. In December, a little bud would burst into a seed that looked just like popcorn. North Florida really had a beautiful fall. The leaves of the maples, dogwoods, sweetgums, a variety of oaks, sumacs, wild cherry trees, and popcorn trees turn a myriad of yellows and reds provided a colorful fall. It was still a little early for a total burst of color, however.

As she walked the trail twice with the boys, Jamie wondered why she wasn't exhausted after all the excitement last night and the strenuous exercise this morning? She showered, dressed, and went to the kitchen for some lunch.

"Junith called. She's coming by in a few minutes," Em relayed through her yawns.

"Want some lunch?" Jamie asked.

"In a minute. I need to finish up these last few pages. I think I just about figured it out."

Jamie called Vonnie so see how she was doing as she prepared lunch.

"Hi, Vonnie. What's new?"

"I have a squirrel visiting the feeder you put up outside my window. He doesn't look very old but he's eaten about half of the corn on the cob."

"Oh, good. It took long enough to get his attention," Jamie noted.

"The helper just came in to take me down to get my hair done," Vonnie said.

"Ok. Talk to you later," Jamie said as she made a mental note to get Vonnie a hummingbird feeder for her window.

Jamie put some bacon on to fry and chopped up some tomatoes, lettuce, artichokes, feta cheese, beets, carrots, onions, and oranges. She crumbled the bacon over the top and made some mustard vinaigrette dressing. Junith arrived just as the cranberry nut muffins, fresh whole wheat bread, sweet tea and the salad were placed on the kitchen table.

"Great timing, Junith. Want some lunch?" Jamie smiled at her. She looked tired, too.

"Yum. Yes, I do." The three of them looked like death warmed over. They looked at each other and just burst out laughing.

"Em, you know Junith and I are getting a little old for this. But, you're young. What's your excuse for looking so hung over?" Jamie teased.

"It tires me out taking care of you old ladies," she mused.

"Junith, what have you found out about Joe's death?" Jamie asked turning to serious matters.

"He was shot with a .38, he had been dead approximately two hours before he was found, and he had eaten a hamburger and fries just before he was shot."

"No idea who killed him?" she asked.

"No idea whatsoever. His office is isolated. No one saw any vehicle other than his truck outside and no one saw anyone else, other than you, enter the building. So, he must have left there on his own accord," she explained.

"There was someone in the back while I was there," Jamie told her.

"Yes, but we can't figure out who it was. We don't know who set the fire to your kennel, nor do we know who is sending you warnings or who is taking pot shots at you. I'm not even sure what you are doing to aggravate the person who is doing this to you." Junith was extremely frustrated and Jamie guessed she hadn't helped matters any.

"Junith," Em began quietly, "not to change the subject but, I may have a situation where a company changed figures on an annual report to its stock holders. I'm the only one who will notice, other than the person who altered the numbers. What do you think? Should I say something about it?"

"Speaking as a law enforcement officer, I would say yes, you should. How much of a stink you should make about it depends on how altered the numbers are. If a company is deep in the red and reports itself in the black, that's one thing. If it is a small alteration, that's something else."

"It's pretty big."

"Just be careful. The person who changed the numbers is not going to be happy about the fact that you noticed," Junith warned.

They cleaned up the lunch dishes. Em went back to her work in the study to e-mail the company about the change. Junith left to go back to her office, and Jamie decided she would help Junith in solving this mystery since there hadn't been much progress made. It appeared to be her fault that there was a mystery at all. She started with the threatening messages.

Who could be sending these messages? Someone had to either have access to a computer with a modem at home or at work. Brookdale was small and the list of computer literate people must also be small. There were computers at the Sheriff's Department and at the library, but where else? Agnes would know.

"Em, I am going over to Joyner's to see Agnes. I shouldn't be gone too long." Em waved without looking up from her work.

Fred's mom was not feeling well so they played three games of Spite and Malice, a favorite north woods game. Vonnie beat Jamie two out of three games. Jamie left after an hour with a list of items to bring back the next trip.

On the way to the crossroads, Jamie passed the road into the Livingston's property. She drove slowly to see if there had been any more progress on the road. There had not been any more work on the road bed but there was a mass of tire tracks all over the place. Maybe the surveyors had been out to determine where to put the main building.

Minor and Jamie entered Joyner's Café and walked up to the counter. Minor, of course, went behind the counter and had a seat. "Hi, Agnes. How's it going?" Jamie asked.

"Good. The lunch crowd just about wiped out my daily special. There's a little left if you want some."

"Thanks but I think I'll just have some sweet tea." She was served a glass of tea and Minor was served a big hunk of ham.

"Agnes, know anybody who has a computer in Brookdale?" Jamie asked.

"Well, let me see now. They have computers over at the library and down at the school because my niece uses one to do her schoolwork. The only other place I know that has one is the post office."

"The post office has a computer?"

"Oh, yes," Agnes responded. "It was a big deal when it came in. It can somehow communicate with other post offices. Johnny, my nephew was telling me about it. You know he delivers the mail on the south side of the county. They get messages from Tallahassee, even Washington, DC. It's really something."

"Does Johnny know how to use it?"

"Nah. He's a simple-minded boy. He does good to get the mail to the right house. Tammie is the only one what knows how to use it."

It was time for Agnes to start preparing the supper special so Minor and Jamie left, albeit with a large soup bone for Major. She drove over to the library to see what types of computers were accessible to the public.

Minor was not welcomed in the library so he was left in the truck with the windows down. Miss Swindemann was at her desk. She had run the Dora Public Library for the past 40 years. "Hello, Miss Swindemann. How are you today?" Jamie asked.

She looked up from her work. "Oh, hello, Jamie," she responded. "I'm very well, thank you. What can I do for you today?" Jamie asked her about computers and public accessibility and was shown the computerized checkout system for the books, which included ten powerful IBM clones all of which had a modem and access to the Internet. Teenagers were seated at all but one of the machines. Jamie was really quite surprised at the number of computers, as well as the power of the machines for this small rural county.

Mrs. Swindemann explained that the machines were obtained from a federal grant for rural development two years ago. The library was automated, the latest computer equipment purchased and an Internet account was established for five years. After that point, the county had to pay for Internet usage.

"Do the machines get much use?" Jamie inquired.

"Oh, yes. The junior high and high students use them all the time after school and on Sunday afternoons. I allow them to play their games on Sunday on all the machines except this one. I leave it in case someone wants to use the Internet."

"Okay if I use that one for a while?"

"Sure. I've been trying to get folks other than students and teachers to use the machines. So many people are scared of computers. I wish I knew a way to get more people in here on these machines." She walked me over to the machine. "Let me know if you need some help," she said as she went back to her desk.

She sat down at the computer to surf the net. The power of the computer systems at Brookdale's library amazed and totally flabbergasted Jamie. To think that Miss Swindemann knew how to use all of these systems. She must be 70 years old. Very few 70-year old ladies knew how to use a computer much less operate on the information highway.

Jamie pulled up the Internet provider's e-mail system called mailer. It was a simple operation using the software program installed on the machine. Anyone with simple computer skills could have e-mailed that warning. She glanced around the computer section at the teenagers. They appeared to be proficient on the machines. Anyone of them could have sent a warning message. She shut down the powerful computer and walked over to the aged-librarian to ask a few more investigative questions.

"Miss Swindemann, in the last week, has the Internet capable computer been used very much?"

"Oh, my yes. It stays busy. You see, students come in to do reports and research papers. They can look up the material by subject on the system and then print out a great deal of information. They can even cut and paste information right into their papers on a word processor program. So, it is very popular."

"Has someone other than students been using the machine lately?" she asked.

"Let me think. Sometimes the teachers from the high school come by to use it and Sheriff Wilson came by the other day. That very nice Mr. McNabb came by to do some research on the stock market. Other than that, I can't think of anyone."

Jamie bristled. So Mr. McNabb had been by. "Do you remember what day Mr. McNabb came by?"

"Now that is the same question the Sheriff asked. It just so happens that I do keep a record of who uses the machine. I sign each user in and out and write the time. It's part of the grant. We have to show how many people use it and how often it is used. Mr. McNabb used the machine from 8 a.m. until 9:24 am last Friday.

"Thank you Miss Swindemann. You've been very helpful. If you need someone to teach a class on the use of the computers, just let me know. I'd be happy to volunteer sometime."

"That's very good of you, Jamie. I may just call you." She smiled sweetly and waved goodbye. Jamie wondered what Ma Pellen saw menacing in the nice old lady's eyes.

It was almost 4 p.m., too late to check the post office. As Jamie and Minor drove up to the house, she noticed Charlie was in the exercise pen in the kennel. That was strange. He was in the house with Em when Jamie had left and her car was still in the driveway. Jamie wondered what was up?

Minor and Jamie walked into the house. "Em," she called. No one answered. Jamie walked into every room but did not find her. Her computer was on, her worked scattered on the desk, but no Em.

"Em," Jamie yelled from the back porch. No answer. She ran over to the kennel, feeling panicked but not knowing why. The alarm system was still on inside the kennel so she wasn't in there. Maybe she just took a walk around the circuit. But, she would have taken Charlie. Something was wrong. Now, Jamie really panicked. Maybe it was all the weird events of the past week or maybe she was paranoid, but she felt that something was very wrong. Jamie called Junith.

"Junith, Em is gone," she said quickly.

"So, she's free, white and 21," was Junith's smart mouthed reply.

"Something is not right. Come over here right away," Jamie said and hung up the phone. It took Junith less than ten minutes to get to the house. Jamie ran out of the house when she drove up.

"What is all this concern about something being wrong?" Junith said as she slowly pulled herself out of the car.

"I left Em about 1 p.m. to go into town. She was working at the computer when I left. When I got home, Charlie was in the pen and there was no sign of Em. She left her computer on, which is something she never does. It looks like she was just interrupted."

She showed Junith the computer, Em's desk and then walked out to get Charlie. Once he was on a leash, Junith said, "Let's see if he has an idea of where she is."

Charlie took off immediately, down the trail toward the Livingston property. They ran after him across the creek and to the road. He seemed to lose the scent at the road. He ran around and around in circles, barking and going nuts.

"That's it. She must have gotten into a vehicle. There are so many tire tracks, I can't even tell what's freshest," Junith said. They walked back to the house, pulling a very determined Charlie back home. "Check your e-mail. See if you have any weird messages."

Jamie hurriedly signed on and checked for any messages. Nothing. They looked at Em's desk and her computer. There were no clues as to what interrupted her.

"What do we do, Junith?" Jamie asked.

"Was anyone scheduled to come out?" Junith inquired.

"Yes. A Mr. McNabb. He called this morning saying he was going to bring his dog out. Em stayed here working and said she would handle it while I went to town. Let's go see if his dog is in the kennel."

They walked out to kennel just as a car drove up. It was an elderly man with a Pitbull. Maybe this was McNabb. Jamie looked at Junith questioningly. She nodded. This was him, all right.

"Good afternoon, ladies. This is Thor." As McNabb walked toward them with Thor on a leash, the dog growled ferociously and pulled on the leash. Junith stayed where she was as Jamie walked toward him to see if Thor was going to calm down. He didn't. McNabb pulled on the leash, and yelled, "Down, Thor." The dog ignored him. The dog pulled at the leash, barked and growled at Jamie and then lunged for her. McNabb barely had the dog under control, and indeed, seemed to enjoy the dog's aggression toward Jamie.

Jamie took a step back and said, "I'm sorry, Mr. McNabb. I will not be able to board your dog due to his violent behavior."

McNabb looked at Jamie incredulously. "What? He's not aggressive. He's just trying to protect me from strangers. He's never bitten anyone."

"That may be true. However, it is my policy to refuse boarding to dogs that act aggressive toward me in any way. There are other kennels nearby. You might want to try one of them."

"Well, I never! I certainly don't see how you expect to run a business by turning away customers. I will take my business to someone who understands and can handle dogs. Good day." He loaded Thor back into his car and took off, spinning his tires in the gravel.

As Jamie turned back toward Junith, she noticed a slight grin. She inwardly admitted that she was glad Junith had been there for this incident. McNabb looked like he could have gotten violent himself.

"What are we going to do about Em?" Jamie asked as if to change the subject.

"WE aren't going to do anything. I am going to get Deputy Clyde and the K-9 unit and search for her. You need to stay here and let me know if she comes back."

13

The airport in Cairo had been backed up since the hotel blew up. Getting to Paris had been a real ordeal. To get out of Cairo, Fred had to buy a first class ticket to Amman on Egypt Air, a bus to Tel Aviv, and then Air France to Paris. Once in Paris, he picked up a Delta ticket back to the states.

Upon arrival in Paris, he checked into the Paris Hilton near the Eiffel Tower and slept for about four hours. He awoke completely fresh and alert so he dressed and took the metro to an area near the Sorbonne and bought some books in French, Spanish, Croatian and Arabic. He probably needed to get a six months supply to keep the languages in tact. He then went to Jeune Gilbert's, a huge book store on Boulevard St. Michel. Inside were books, tapes, videos, magazines and more. He had fun as he walked around such a well-stocked store. He felt a little guilty but enjoyed himself tremendously.

Once loaded down with several kilos of books, he stopped by Fauchon's to buy Jamie some chocolates. She especially liked the chocolate covered cherries that have the stem sticking out the top while inside the seed is floating in brandy. One last stop at the French deli near the Hilton to load up with fresh bread, cheese and wine, and he went back to the hotel room.

Once inside his room, he dropped everything on the bed and called Jamie. It was now 6 a.m. in Brookdale, so he knew Jamie would be up.

"Hello."

"Hi, Jamie. I'm in Paris."

"Oh, Fred. I was so worried about you. Are you all right?"

"I'm fine," he assured me.

"Were the bookstores open?" Sometimes the French take bank holidays at the most unexpected times.

"Yes. I just got back from shopping. I bought more books than I'll need. I found a bunch of Simenon's Maigret series so I'll be set for awhile. How's everything there?"

"Em is missing." She explained what happened.

"Let Junith and Clyde handle it. Don't go out exploring. You cannot do more than they are already doing. I mean it."

"I know. I just wish there was something I could do. I'm so worried about her. I cannot imagine anyone getting close enough to her to kidnap her with her black belt in Taekwondo."

"She can take care of herself. I'll be home tomorrow on Delta's flight 1241 from Atlanta at 6 p.m."

"I'll be at the airport at 5 just in case you're early. I've really missed you."

"I've missed you too. I'll see you tomorrow. Take care of yourself. Make sure the boys are in the house with you."

"What about the fleas?"

"I can live with the fleas, but I can't live without you."

"I love you."

"Me too. Bye."

If Fred wasn't going to be home until tomorrow, Jamie had all day to try to find Em. She fixed breakfast and tried to figure out why anyone would kidnap Em. What would they gain? Did Em see something she shouldn't have? She had talked about some discrepancies in a report she had written. Did that have something to do with her kidnapping? With coffee and muffin in hand, Jamie sat down to check her mail and to use the word processor to make a list in hopes it would clarify her thinking.

There were no new e-mail messages. Em must have seen something. Maybe she took a walk around the circuit and saw something on the Livingston property. No, she would have taken Charlie. There must be some clue.

Jamie walked over and sat at Em's computer that was still on. She had been afraid to turn it off in case something significant had not been saved. Em's manuscript lay open to page 231 with all its red penciled editorial comments. The computer screen was filled with a list of missing or conflicting information that the author would need to correct or supply. Could Jamie check Em's e-mail?

She pulled up her e-mail software package. Em used hotmail for her mail. She had her username and password on a yellow sticky on her computer screen. Jamie typed it in. There were several messages from the author of the manuscript she was working on and one from her publisher. Of course, if she sent a message, it wouldn't be here unless she saved a copy. Jamie opened the folder where Em saved her e-mail messages. Sure enough, there was a message to the company which had a discrepancy. She opened it and read it.

> *Jonothan, there seems to be a problem with your annual report. Please contact me ASAP.*

The message was sent at 2:13 p.m. Maybe Jonathan called and set up a meeting. Jamie sat there with her hands in her lap, and felt helpless.

She looked over at the answering machine. It was not blinking. It struck her as strange that it was not blinking when she arrived home yesterday. Seldom does an afternoon pass without a call from someone. Maybe Em had taken a call. Jamie walked over and looked at the message book. Nothing. She pressed the play button, just for kicks, to listen to the last message recorded. She was shocked to hear someone who sounded a lot like herself.

"Em, this is Jamie. I'm calling from my cellular. I'm over on the Livingston property, just across the creek. Come over here fast. Don't bring Charlie. He'll make too much noise. Hurry, up." Then, there was just a click. Jamie called Junith immediately. She was out but Deputy Clyde was there so Jamie told him about the call.

"Bring the tape by the office so Junith can hear it when she gets back," he ordered. Jamie grabbed the whole answering machine with the tape and headed to the Sheriff's Office.

Junith pulled into the parking lot just as Jamie got out of the truck. They walked into the small office together. Junith and Clyde listened intently to the tape. Junith spoke first, "That's not you but it sure is close to being you. Any idea who this is?"

"No. And, why would someone lure Em to that property, anyway?" Jamie's voice quivered, showing just how scared she was. Junith and Clyde picked up on her nervousness immediately.

"Look, Jamie," Junith began, "at least someone kidnapped her. They could have shot her and left her on the ground. They took her alive and I'm sure she still is alive. We'll keep this tape. Take your player, go home and turn on your system. Keep a gun close by and don't go meeting anyone on the Livingston property."

"Fred's coming home tomorrow. I'm picking him up at 6:00. Other than that, I plan to stay home. Let me know if you need me." Jamie looked questioningly into Junith's stony grey eyes but got nothing from them. "Bye," Jamie said angrily and walked out of the office. She was more than a little dazed by the events that surrounded Em's disappearance. Through the window of the Sheriff's Office she could see that Junith was on the phone. Junith knows something about Em that she's not telling. Jamie grew angrier.

Jamie spent the rest of the day in the kennel. She exercised and tried to relax. The excitement of Fred's return, Em's disappearance and the anger she felt toward Junith made it hard to relax.

That night, Jamie turned to her other mode of relaxing: cooking. She sliced onions until tears welled up in her eyes. She was not convinced it was just the onions. She used a modified recipe from an old cookbook by Julia Childs to prepare a pot of French onion soup. She focused on the menu and Fred's arrival, and eventually, her anger subsided. But, her concern for Em was still foremost in her mind. Her anger towards Junith was totally forgotten.

Fred liked French onion soup granitee after a long flight. The meal made for a simple but hearty supper when you're tired. She put the wine, onion, butter and beef mixture in the crock pot so it could simmer all night.

The night passed without incident and basically without sleep. Early on, she attempted to enter data on her spreadsheet that housed her kennel accounts, but got distracted and nearly deleted her whole file.

Around midnight, Jamie flipped around 50 stations on the TV, but nothing interested her. She was too nervous to read anything serious. She picked up a Perry Mason mystery that always relaxed her, but she couldn't focus on it. Her last attempt to force herself to sleep was to play a P.G Wodehouse tape of the Jeeves series. This usually put her right to sleep, but not on this night. Finally, she decided to just lay there and hoped sleep would finally come. She looked at the clock. It was 3:30 a.m. At 5:00, she got up.

Jamie made some of Fred's favorite muffins, banana nut oat bran, and put some wheat bread mix in the bread machine. After an hour cleaning up the house, she went out to work in the kennel.

The morning flew past as she cleaned the kennel and exercised the dogs. By noon, her stomach had begun to growl. She showered again and decided to go to Joyner's for lunch. This would be the third meal there in a week. Oh well, the exercise would take care of all that cholesterol, she lied to herself.

Minor and Jamie entered Joyner's. The place was about half full. Minor headed behind the counter. Jamie grabbed a newspaper from the bar, said hello to Agnes, and ordered the special. When Agnes brought the plate that was mounded higher than usual, she asked, "Have you heard anything from Em?" Tears glazed over Jamie's eyes. Word sure traveled fast around this town. She just shook her head no. "Em can take care of herself, honey. Don't worry about her," she announced then went back to the kitchen.

Jamie ate the large mound of fried, greasy, delicious food, greedily. She didn't remember eating supper last night. Maybe that's why she couldn't sleep. She read every word in the newspaper, all about the talented, but losing high school football team, the death notices, the birth notices, the comics, Ann Landers, her horoscope, and the classifieds. Time to move on. She gathered up Minor, a bone for Major and paid the bill.

"Fred coming home soon?" Agnes asked.

"Today," Jamie said with a forced smile. "About time, huh?"

"Good." That's all she said and turned to wait on a customer.

Jamie would have to leave Brookdale by 4:30 p.m. to make sure she was in Tallahassee to pick up Fred by 6. She considered taking Minor but decided against it. Before leaving, she turned on all the alarms and packed her .38.

The trip to Tallahassee could be made in one of two ways. She could either take I-10 which was a longer distance but four-laned where she could travel at 70 mph. Or, she could travel on Highway 20 that was a shorter route but was two-laned and curvy so passing slow cars or trucks was impossible or life threatening, resulting in an average speed of 45 mph. She had plenty of time so she took Highway 20.

The BBC World News was on WFSU FM 88.9. Jamie enjoyed this news cast because of the detailed information but also enjoyed the British accent. Today's world report was about the Russian Mafia. In lieu of a strong police force, the Mafia had taken over many of the profitable economic ventures in Russia such as the drug market, and the black market for imported goods since the advent of capitalism and democracy. The organization was so strong and powerful that it had begun to infiltrate into the US, overpower the present Mafia in cities such as Chicago and New York. Well, at least that's something the citizens of Brookdale didn't have to worry about.

Jamie arrived at the airport in plenty of time, parked in the short term parking area, and walked down to the Delta gate. A large crowd of people waited to depart on the next flight. She sat across from the gate and watched as the plane landed right on schedule. After a few minutes, she moseyed up to the door until she stood right in the doorway. Fred was the third one off the plane. She grabbed him and held on tight. All the suppressed emotions came out at once. Tears rolled down her cheeks.

They walked as one to the baggage claim area. They didn't talk, but clung to each other. Fred retrieved his bags and they walked out to the truck.

Jamie and Fred drove down Highway 20, heading home. Fred talked about his trip, his research, the blowing up of the hotel, the confusion afterwards, Paris, and his uneventful flight home. It was his way of winding down. Jamie listened intently.

They pulled into the driveway about 7:30 p.m. It was still light. Jamie let Minor and Major out to welcome Fred home. He had brought them a treat of airline food.

She sat on the bed as Fred unpacked. "Here. This is from Cairo," he said as he handed Jamie a small package wrapped in white tissue paper. Jamie opened the jewelry box to find a cartouche pendant. It was not just any cartouche, but her Arabic name (Amira) written in hieroglyphics.

"Oh, baby, it's beautiful." She jumped up and hugged him.

"You know they make these while you wait, now. Remember back in the '80's when you had to wait 2 weeks to get a ring made? It's amazing to watch them. I'm glad you like it. It's the "new" style of cartouche. They seem to have a different style about every 2 years. Here. This is from Paris," he announced as he threw Jamie a package.

"I know what this is...chocolates from Fauchon's." She quickly ripped open the package. "Oh, Fred. Not those chocolate covered cherries with the stems sticking out." She bit into one as the liquor ran down her chin. "They are decadent. Want one?" They each ate four liquor soaked cherries.

"What's for supper?" Fred asked.

"Now, what do you think?" Jamie responded.

"French onion soup with crusty cheese," Fred said.

"In five minutes."

As they sat down to eat, Fred asked, "So, what's been happening here?" Jamie filled him in on everything that had happened since he had been gone, even what he had already heard. He sat quietly and listened.

"I'm tired right now. but tomorrow call Junith. See if she and Mark can come over for dinner. I want to talk to her about this property and harassment. But right now, I need a melatonin to help me get a good night's sleep."

Jamie hadn't felt sleepy, but with Fred's arms around her, she fell asleep immediately and woke up ten hours later. Fred, of course, had been up at 4 a.m., his body's clock being all confused due to international travel. By the time she got up, he had breakfast cooked, the boys fed, and had made a list of things "to do". They ate breakfast watching the news. CNN was reporting on the situation in Russia as capitalism and democracy were being pushed on the Russians. The newscast reiterated the story Jamie had heard on the way to the airport. Evidently, the Russian Mafia had branch offices around the world to launder its money from drug sales and other illegal activities.

Fred reacted to this news cast. "The problem is we made capitalism sound too easy and too good. We forced capitalism and democracy on these people but forgot to tell them about the sacrifices they would need to make. They had to give up the security of government jobs. Even though it was a low paying job, at least they had a job," he lectured.

Jamie looked at Fred. It always felt so good to have him back home after a absence. Jamie really did not like being away from him. It made her feel "incomplete" somehow. They had always been a team, which made it hard to operate without each other. He must have heard her thinking. He said, "I missed you Jamie. It's no fun away from you. Next time, you come with me, kennel or no kennel." She just smiled.

He turned off the TV and picked up his list. "Look. Come here. Two fleas on my arm. Look!"

"I don't see anything," she said smiling. He just rolled his eyes as he slapped his arm and looked at her. Jamie ignored him.

Changing the subject, Fred said, "Okay, today I want to find out who killed Joe and put him in our house, who tried to burn down your kennel, where Em is hiding out, who killed that Georgia kid and buried him beside the river, and what is happening on the land beside us."

"Forget the Georgia kid, let's work on finding Em!"

"You're right. The most important thing is to find Em. Let's go over everything about her disappearance again." It took about fifteen minutes to cover her disappearance. "Clearly someone has kidnapped her, but why?"

Junith drove up and Jamie met her at the door. "Good morning, Junith. Had breakfast yet?"

"Yeah. But, I could stand another cup of coffee. Welcome back, Fred. I tried my hardest to keep her out of trouble but you know she has a real knack for finding it."

"I know. I want to talk to you about Em. I have some ideas."

Jamie handed Junith a cup of strong black coffee and said, "While you two talk, I'm going to run out to the kennel so I'll be ready to help out once y'all figure out what to do." She walked out on the porch. "Come on, boys. Let's go to the kennel and feed the rest of the guys."

14

The sun was up but behind some light clouds. The morning was fresh with just a hint of briskness in the air. The birds were chirping. All seemed so right with the world but so much was so wrong. Where was Em? There must be some clue that was being overlooked. Jamie was so intent on her thoughts as she opened the door of the kennel that "Oh!" was all she could say. Em was on the floor wrapped securely in a blanket. She bent down and checked her pulse. Em was alive but her heartbeat was not a strong one. She must be drugged. Jamie ran screaming from the kennel to the back of the house.

"I found Em! Call an ambulance. Hurry!"

Fred called 911 as Junith ran back to the kennel with Jamie. "Don't move her. Wait for the ambulance," she instructed. Jamie brushed Em's hair back from her face and held her hand. She did not move. Junith checked her pockets. She found a piece of paper. She read it and put it in her pocket.

"What does it say?" Jamie asked.

"Nothing," Junith replied.

"Junith, tell me," Jamie pleaded.

"You don't need to know. It will only get you in trouble."

"Well, next time I'll search the pockets before calling you." She looked at her with a great deal of disgust. Junith looked at her and handed her the note which read: "*We could have easily killed her but we didn't. She'll be fine in a few days.*" Fred joined them in the kennel.

After a long fifteen minutes the ambulance arrived. The orderlies put Emily on a stretcher. "I'll go to the hospital with her. Fred, would you please feed the dogs for me? I'll call as soon as she wakes up."

"Ok," Fred said. He hugged her briefly and she climbed into the ambulance.

Once at the hospital, they wheeled Em through the emergency room doors and disappeared into never-never land. Jamie was stopped and asked to fill out the paperwork. Paperwork seemed so mundane in a time of crisis. Em could die while Jamie filled out papers and provided uniformed personnel with her address and telephone number. It seemed ironic to Jamie. If Em died, what difference did it make? If she lived, they could ask her for the information. Fred had handed her Em's purse as she had climbed aboard the ambulance. He sure thought straight during an emergency.

Jamie took out Em's insurance card and license, wrote down all the "vital" information on the thousand forms she had been given and then asked to go back to be with her. The lady who took the forms called for the doctor to come talk to her.

"You'll need to sign this one last form," said the admitting personnel.

"What is it?" Jamie asked.

"Just a routine form saying you are the person bringing in the patient," she replied without looking at Jamie.

Jamie read the form. It stated that by signing, Jamie would be responsible for all bills incurred by the patient. Jamie put a big "NO WAY" on the form and walked off.

A woman in a green coat and pants came to the door. Jamie looked at her and faintly recognized her. Susie Rightford. They had grown up together in DeSoto City but were never really close friends. She had married a guy from Brookdale. Jamie did not know she worked at Dora County Hospital. "Hello, Jamie."

"Hi, Susie. How's Em?"

"I can tell you this much. She has been drugged but is otherwise okay. The drugs are not dangerous but she will sleep for awhile. If you want to go home, I'll call you when Em comes to. We can't tell for certain, but she'll probably be out for eight or ten hours."

"No, I'd rather stay beside her."

"How did she get drugged?" she asked.

"Sheriff Wilson will be by shortly to write up a report for the hospital. The drugs were not self-induced," Jamie offered as some sort of explanation.

"I'm glad to hear that. Em is not the sort of person you'd expect to overdose on drugs. I've got to run, but first, I'll show you where she is and where the coffee pot is located."

After a brief detour to the coffee corner, they entered Em's room. "There she is. Make yourself comfortable," Susie instructed and then left. Jamie tried to get comfortable in the hospital chair next to her bed. She couldn't sit still. She had so many questions that only Em could answer and she felt so guilty about her condition.

Jamie glanced at her watch. Three hours had already gone by. Time stood still during emergencies. It was 11 a.m. and Em had not moved a muscle during the time she was with her. Jamie called home to tell Fred and Junith the situation.

At noon, Fred and Junith entered the room with a bag of books and sandwiches. "How's the patient?" Fred asked.

"She looks peaceful enough. Someone checks her vital signs every thirty minutes. They are getting stronger every time they are checked. Look at the chart at the end of the bed."

As Junith and Fred looked at the chart, the door opened. All you could see was a mass of yellow roses. An orderly placed the roses on the beside table. "Roses for Ms. Rosini," he said with a smile. There must have been three dozen roses in that vase.

As the orderly left, Junith opened and read the card. "Sorry to inconvenience you. Hope you have a speedy recovery." It was not signed.

"Sounds like someone has a guilty conscience," Junith said. They are from the Flowers, Etc. shop here in Brookdale. Junith walked to the phone and called David Johnson, the owner of the shop.

"Hello. May I please speak to David?" she asked. "David, this is Junith. How are you? Good. Listen, you just sent three dozen yellow roses to Em Rosini in the hospital. Who paid for them? Uh huh. Uh huh. Okay. Thanks." She hung up. And stared out the window.

"Well?" Jamie asked.

"A long distance caller used a credit card with the name of Meredith Seymour."

"The plot thickens," Fred put in.

"Gotta go. See ya," Junith said as she rushed out of the door.

"Fred, why would anyone kidnap and drug Em?"

"Let's think about it. Think of all the activities she's involved in, her work, the people she knows, and what you two have been up to."

Here we go again, making lists. "In the last week, she has been living with me and working in the kennel. She's stayed at our house except when she went into town to pick up her computer and clothes and a few groceries. Her work is at our house. She was working on a manuscript that is beside her computer. And *we* haven't been *up* to anything."

"Okay. I'm going home to check the manuscript she was working on. I'll be back around 6 with some supper if you don't call before then."

"Please be careful and follow your own advice and turn on the alarm system while you are home," Jamie said as Fred kissed her good-bye and smiled.

"Yes, mam."

Jamie turned on the radio to listen to the news on the half hour. There was a report that detailed Em had been kidnapped and drugged and that the Sheriff's Department was looking into it. Em was not originally from Brookdale, and had only lived here five years, so there was just mild interest in the outsider being a victim. Of course, they did not believe it was one of the locals who committed the crime, either. She switched off the radio and looked at Em.

She wondered if she had gotten Em into something that jeopardized her life? Jamie was wrought with guilt. Em had to be okay. She was going to be okay. Tears started down her eyes. What had they done to her while they had her? Why did they let her go? The tears stopped as suddenly as they had started. Jamie was jolted as though someone had hit her with a rock. How did they get into the kennel without the alarm system going off? She jumped up and called Fred.

"Hello?" His voice was calming.

"Hey, baby. Listen, I turned on the alarm system in the kennel before I went to pick you up. How did they put Em into my kennel without the alarm going off?" Jamie asked.

"You are sure you turned it on?"

"Positive."

"Junith and I assumed you had not turned it on. Was it off when you went in this morning?"

"No. I opened the door, turned off the system and then saw Em."

"The only answer is that someone has a combination that will disengage the system. Did Em have a code?"

"Of course. She needed one to get into the kennel when I was gone."

"Does Em use the same code as you or one especially for her?"

"You know, I figured out it does not matter. I can turn it on with my number and she can turn if off with her number. So, once you give a number out to someone, they can enter and exit at anytime until you take their number out of the system."

"I didn't know that," Fred said cautiously.

"Another thing, we have glass breaks in case a window is broken and the button on the door to determine if a door is opened but we did not put a motion detector in the kennel because of the dogs. If someone entered somehow other than through the door or breaking a window, then the system would not go off. You would think the dogs would bark, though."

"We assumed they entered through the door with no alarm system. I'm going to call Junith and go take a look at the kennel. I'll call you back later."

Time went by slowly for the next four hours. Suddenly, Em moved, ever so slightly. Jamie jumped up and stood beside her. Then, there was a groan. Jamie hit the button for the nurse. She came quickly. "I think she's waking up."

"I'll get the doctor," the nurse said.

Susie arrived in the room in just minutes. Em had moved a little more and groaned but she had not opened her eyes. She took the vital signs and talked to Em stroking her forehead. Jamie's immediate thoughts were that only a female doctor would stroke her head. It is very much a feminine thing. Em opened her eyes. "Where am I?"

Jamie almost laughed. It sounded like a cheap movie line. Susie told Em she was in the hospital and started asking her what her name is, where she lives, and other trivial questions. Em answered but slowly, giving lots of thought to each question.

Focusing her eyes, she looked toward the other side of the bed and said "Hello, Jamie." That was enough for Jamie to tear up.

"What's wrong. What's happened?" she asked.

"Nothing now that you are okay."

"I feel so tired," Em said as she shut her eyes.

"She will be fading in and out for awhile. We need to let her recoup at her own pace. She's going to be fine. She's in excellent health with a strong body. I'm not worried about her recovery."

Susie left and Jamie called Fred to let him know Em had woken up. "She's groggy but Susie said she'll be fine. She just has to let her body handle the drugs. She should be able to come home tomorrow."

"That is good news. I checked the kennel. Someone entered through the exercise pen, went up the ramp of an empty run and into the kennel. Footprints are very clearly defined all the way up to the ramp."

"Just goes to show the alarm system doesn't keep out the professionals."

"Let's meet for supper. Then, I'll go home, feed the dogs, get some fresh clothes and go back to the hospital. I want to stay with Em tonight."

"It's not your fault, Jamie. Don't blame yourself for this."

"She's a good friend. I want to be with her."

"Okay. I'll pick you up at 6."

They pulled into Joyner's about 6:30. It was crowded. Agnes waved them to a booth.

"Welcome back stranger," Agnes said to Fred. She sat down two scotches on the rocks. "I assume you both need a drink after finding Em."

"You're right on the mark, Agnes," Fred said smiling. "Here's a trinket from Egypt."

She opened the packaged wrapped in tissue paper. "Oh, it's beautiful," she exclaimed as she pulled out a gold bangle with inscriptions written around it.

"It is your name in hieroglyphics, the ancient Egyptian writing," Fred explained.

"I'm going to bring you both a big plate of food. You two just sit and relax." As she walked off, Fred just stared at her.

"Agnes seems to anticipate everyone's needs. How does she do it?" he asked.

"It's called a mothering instinct. Some women and even some men have it," Jamie said smiling.

Agnes returned with a plate of lamb shanks, turnip greens, mashed potatoes and gravy, and a tomato-cucumber salad. Fred and Jamie ate hungrily in silence until they were stuffed.

Just as they ate the last bit of gravy with a biscuit, two apple pie a la modes arrived with black coffee, one decaf, one regular. "Gosh, you don't even have to talk here. Just think it and it appears," Fred said. They finished off the pie and second cup of coffee as Agnes came over to the table with her bracelet on her arm.

"I hear Em is doing okay. Any word on what happened?" she asked.

"Not yet. Susie said to hold the questions until tomorrow but she is coming around. I'm headed back that way now," Jamie replied.

"Let me fix a plate of food in case she wakes up. There's nothing worth eating at that hospital." She sent them off with a huge plate of food and a jug of sweet tea.

Em was sitting up in her bed when Jamie entered the hospital room. She looked a little glassy eyed but smiled weakly. "Hey, partner. How ya doin?" Her speech was a little slurred but she was obviously getting better, thank God.

"Agnes sent you some food. Do you feel like eating?"

"I sure do. Hand it over." She ate hungrily. Jamie watched her quietly thinking to herself how she would have felt if Em had not recovered. Tears came to her eyes about the time Em looked up. "Hey, I'm fine. What are the tears for?"

"I was so worried about you. I'm just thankful you are okay," Jamie managed to say through sobs and tears.

"Me, too," she said in a stronger voice than before. Agnes' food seemed to help.

The door to the room opened and Junith walked in. "Well, don't we look better."

"We certainly feel better," Em replied.

"What happened to you?" Junith asked.

"I was working at the computer. I had gone out to the kennel to work. On the way back into the house, I heard the phone ring but didn't make it in time to catch it. I listened to the message on the answering machine. It was from Jamie. She wanted me to meet her at the Creek on the Livingston property without Charlie. I put him up and walked over to the creek. I didn't see Jamie or her car so I crossed the creek. Just as I walked out of the woods onto the new road over there, I blacked out. I have no idea what happened after that until I woke up here in this room."

"Did someone grab you?" Junith asked.

"I don't remember, but normally, I have automatic reflexes to avoid being grabbed with my training in Taekwondo. So, I would say no, no one grabbed me."

"You still look weak. I'll come by tomorrow and we'll talk some more," Junith said as she started to leave.

"I'm going to take her home as soon as Susie comes by to look at her again. Call the house before you come out here," Jamie told her. She gave her two fingered salute. Just before she closed the door, Junith popped back in to ask Em if she knew a Meredith Seymour. Em said she had never heard the name.

After the food and the questioning, Em politely rolled over and went to sleep. So much for going home tonight. Jamie did not want to leave her alone in case someone had ideas about walking into the hospital to harm her. Jamie removed her .38 from her purse and placed it in her lap. She sat in the chair and read with one eye and watched the door with the other. It made for a long night.

Em woke up bright and early. Susie came in at 6 a.m., and gave her the go ahead to leave after she told her about any lingering symptoms she might encounter, mainly weakness and drowsiness.

Jamie called Fred from the truck to let him know they were on the way home. They arrived about 7:30. Junith's car was in the drive. Em stopped at the exercise pen to let Charlie out so Jamie brought Major and Minor out, too. Fred had a huge breakfast ready for them as they walked in the door. The three dogs stayed on the back porch with a treat as the humans chowed down in the kitchen.

They stuffed themselves with food, cleared the table and decided to take the dogs for a short walk. Fred talked about Egypt, Em talked about the hospital, and Junith and Jamie just listened. They laughed and enjoyed the walk. When they entered the house, they sat down to a serious discussion about what had happened to Em, why it had happened, and how to prevent it from happening again.

"Do you remember anything from the time you left the creek to the time you woke up in the hospital?" Junith asked.

"It seems as though I heard a man's voice but it is such a vague recollection, I cannot be sure," Em admitted. "I don't remember "seeing" anything but I remember smelling farm smells like chickens or something."

Junith noted Em's answers in her little black book and stared at Em. She had hoped she would have more to say.

"I'm sorry, but nothing else is in my head. Susie said I may remember more as time goes by. If I do, I'll call you, okay?" Em was a little exasperated. She wanted to help so much but just couldn't.

"No hurry. Just let me know if you remember anything else." Junith was trying to soothe her. "Listen, we have several possibilities. I don't want to move on any one of them until I have a little more information. I'm watching all the leads very carefully so when we are ready to move, we will know exactly where everyone is."

"Em, you look really tired. Why don't you go rest a while and I'll go take care of the kennel," Jamie suggested.

"You're right. I am pooped. Thanks for everything, Jamie." She gave her a smile and headed for the bedroom.

"Junith, what can I do to help?" Jamie asked.

"Stay out of it, basically. This is police work, Jamie. I have Deputy Clyde to help me. We are close to figuring this thing out. I don't want you to end up like Em or Joe so just stay out of it." Her voice was almost threatening. Jamie just looked her in the eyes and said nothing. Junith rose to leave. Fred walked her to her car as Jamie veered off to the kennel.

"Junith, what do you think about this McNabb guy? Could he have had anything to do with it?" Fred asked.

"I've been looking into it. He has an alibi. He was eating at Joyner's during the time Em disappeared."

"Why don't you and Mark come over for dinner on Friday? I brought back a few bottles of Omar Khayyam wine and even a couple bottles of Egyptian Stella beer."

"Sounds great. I'll check with Mark and let you know for sure by tonight."

Fred waved goodbye to Junith and walked to the kennel to see if Jamie needed any help. He found her sitting on a stack of dog food staring into space. He sat down beside her and put his arm around her shoulders. "It's okay, baby. Em's fine and Junith is getting close to clearing up the problem."

"I just feel exhausted, Fred. I don't know what I'm doing wrong to make someone violent. Someone is misreading my actions. But, who? I really believe we need to look closer at the computer messages. That's the real clue."

"You could be right. With Em being kidnapped, we have slighted that aspect."

"Could you feed the dogs for me? I want to go in town to the post office."

"Or, we could do the kennels together and go into town together," he suggested.

"No, that would leave Em alone. I'd rather one of us stayed home with her." Fred reluctantly agreed to do the kennel chores while Jamie went into town. She also needed to pick up Mrs. White's poodle for boarding.

She pulled up to the post office at about 11:00. The center of the little town was bustling with activity. There was even a line at the one window of the post office. Jamie waited behind Mary Ann Schofield. "Hi, Jamie. How are you?"

"Hello, Mary Ann. Fine. How are you?"

"Good. Jamie, why don't you join Brookdale's Women's Club? We would love to have you as a member. In fact, we've got a meeting today at 4:30."

"You know, I just don't have much free time, running the kennel and running after Fred," Jamie said with a smile. She really didn't like women's clubs and had been trying to avoid running into Mary Ann.

"We don't meet that often, Jamie and you're not obliged to come to every meeting or participate in every function. Besides, it would help you make contacts for your business and give you a chance to get out of the house once in awhile. Sometimes it's nice to be with a bunch of women."

She was right, of course. Jamie's grandmother, who lived to be 99, once told her that she had made a mistake early in her retirement by joining bridge clubs of 4 or 8 people. In the end, her grandmother had outlived them all and was stuck playing with people who were not of the same caliber. She said it would have been better if she had joined established "clubs" because clubs did not die like bridge players but were refreshed with new members. This advice was burned into Jamie's mind for some reason.

"You know, you're right, Mary Ann. I really should join," Jamie admitted in a moment of weakness.

"Try to make it this afternoon. Otherwise, we meet the first Tuesday in each month. I'll give you a call to remind you of our next meeting if you cannot make it today," she said happily.

"Okay," Jamie said meekly, already regretting her submission.

"Next, please," Tammie mumbled from the window.

"Talk to you later, Jamie."

She just nodded, and hoped she hadn't made a mistake. She could always bow out later, but it might be good for her.

Then, it was her turn at the window. She was the last in line so she had the opportunity to talk to Tammie for a minute.

"Hello, Tammie," Jamie said.

"Hello, Jamie. What can I do for you?" she asked very professionally.

"I need a book of stamps, please." Jamie looked past her into her office space. On her desk was a computer and printer.

As Tammie retrieved the stamps from a drawer, Jamie added, "Nice computer. Brookdale's post office must do a good business," she said inquiringly.

Tammie just looked at Jamie, grinned slightly, and said, "Yeah, right."

The back door to the office opened and a man with two mail sacks entered.

"Here you go, Tammie. Today's supply of work." He smiled at her before he saw Jamie. He tipped his hat to her and looked like he kinda recognized her, grabbed the outgoing mail bag and asked, "Anything else to go out?"

Jamie recognize Tom. He was a senior the last year she taught at the high school. He had been a bright young man with tremendous promise. Instead, he had chosen to burn his brain out on LSD. He had recuperated back to where he could work in a minimum wage job after putting his family through a great deal of grief and debt.

"Excuse me just a moment, Jamie," she said. "Yes, Tom, there are two packages on the back shelf to go in priority mail."

"Got them. See you tomorrow." He turned to leave, looking at the boxes. "Gosh," he mumbled to himself, "another one overseas?" He walked out the door looking a little puzzled. Tammie looked at him and then turned back to Jamie.

"I also need a couple of stamps for priority mail envelopes." She handed me two stamps. "You know, these stamps fall off. The post office must be cutting back on the budget for glue. I had four different envelopes returned due to lack of postage that I had put on the envelopes myself."

"You want a complaint form?" she asked.

"I have already filled one out. I received a letter saying the glue is of the highest quality most of the time. They enclosed one free stamp. I'm not sure how that compensates me for the four stamps I lost. I thought I was pretty lucky to get one." Tammie just stared blankly at Jamie while she went on about her stamp fiasco.

"Anything else?" Tammie asked when she had finished.

"No, thanks. Have a good one," Jamie said as she turned to walk off. Tammie continued to stare.

As she left the post office, she saw Tom as he waited for the traffic to pass so he could pull out from the post office parking lot. "Tom," Jamie called. He looked her way questioningly. She ran over to the mail truck.

"Yes?" he responded.

"Tom, how are you? Do you remember me? Mrs. Pellen, your English teacher during your senior year?"

"Oh, yeah. Yeah, I do. How are you?"

"Great. I just noticed you looked a little confused when you picked up the packages. You said something about another one going overseas?"

"Yeah. There's usually one or two packages a day either to Washington, D.C. or Moscow, Russia." He stared into space.

"Well, maybe it's a correspondence course or something," Jamie suggested. "Anyway, it was good to see you. You take care." He pulled out and she waved.

As Jamie turned back to her truck, she noticed Tammie moving away from the window of the post office.

Jamie went by to pick up Mrs. White's poodle. Mrs. White came to the door before Jamie could ring the doorbell. "Hello, Jamie. Come in. I have Muffin all ready to go." She picked up Muffin, put her into a carry case with a few toys and a pillow. She added a bag of treats and handed her to Jamie. "You be a good girl," she instructed Muffin.

"Thanks, Mrs. White. You are always so organized and ready when I pick up Muffin. I really appreciate it."

"And I appreciate the great service you provide, Jamie. I'll be back in six days."

"Have a great trip." As she was walking out of her house, Jamie noticed a cluster of Russian dolls on the table beside the door.

"Aren't those cute," she commented. "Where did you get those?"

"Well, I never plan to visit Russia but I did think these are kind of cute. I picked them up over at Jim's Hardware store. They had a few Russian knickknacks. They were not terribly expensive but they give my entry way an international flare, don't you think?"

"Why, yes, I do." She carried Muffin out to the truck and placed her inside the cab. She decided to pulled into Joyner's for a quick cup of coffee and to say hello to Agnes. The place smelled so good. The day's menu consisted of chicken and dumplings, field peas, lettuce and tomato salad with mayonnaise, and apple cobbler. "Hello, Agnes. How are you?"

"Good. How's Em?" she asked.

"I left her at home asleep. Fred's doing my chores for me and keeping an eye on Em while I run errands. She ate your supper down, every bit of it," I relayed.

"She'll be all right. She's a healthy girl," Agnes added.

"Agnes, do you know anything about Tammie?"

"The girl over at the post office?" Agnes asked.

"Yeah. Where's she from?"

"She moved to Brookdale as the post office manager about three years ago just after Sam Martin died in a car accident. He had run the post office for almost thirty-five years. She was relocated from a position in Washington, D.C. We all wondered why somebody local didn't get the job but it is a federal position and anyone could apply."

"Do you know anything about her family?" I asked.

"No, she keeps pretty much to herself. She is very efficient as far as the post office goes. She doesn't have much personality. But, people around here accept people for what they are."

"When did she and Eddie start seeing each other?"

"After his wife left him, he suffered a great deal. Not that he didn't deserve it, the monster that he had been. It took him about six months to recover after he lost his family and job. He met Tammie just after she arrived and got married just about a year later."

"Agnes, I can't stand it. Your lunch smells so good. I'll take three carry outs." Jamie sipped strong black coffee and thought about Tammie as Agnes heaped mounds of food into Styrofoam platters and ham hocks into baggies. Tammie was basically a loner without a past. Jamie's thoughts were interrupted by Mrs. Swindemann.

"Well, hello, Jamie. It is so nice to see you," she cooed.

"How are you Mrs. Swindemann? Everything at the library okay?"

"Yes. Yes, everything is fine. I wanted to set up a computer class for interested folks on Thursday evening. I have a class of ten, one per computer. You mentioned you would help me the other day. Does your offer still stand?"

"Sure. What do you want me to do?" Jamie said politely but groaned inwardly.

"I can do the word processing portion, but I would be grateful if you would show them how to sign onto the Internet."

"No problem. If you'll just make sure everyone has a login script with a working password, I'd be happy to help them go surfing."

"Wonderful. I've also asked Tammie from the post-office to show the group how to send e-mail. So, each of us will spend thirty minutes with the group. I'll let you go first, then Tammie and then I'll take over. So, if you want to leave after your presentation, you may."

"Sounds great. See you Thursday at 5:30." Jamie paid Agnes, picked up her carry out order, and heard Mrs. Swindemann making arrangements for snacks for Thursday night.

Jamie arrived home at noon. As she drove up, she saw Em in the yard playing with Charlie. She looked almost normal but she just didn't have quite the right color to her skin yet. Em walked toward the truck, but Charlie beat her to it and he was in Jamie's face with kisses before she could stop him. "I've got food so please hold Charlie back," she yelled.

"Sit, Charlie," she instructed. He sat immediately and drooled all over the place. "Let me help," Em offered. Em took Muffin and placed her in the kennel while Jamie carried the food into the house.

Fred met Jamie at the door with a smile on his face. "Boy, that sure smells good. I'm glad there's no cholesterol or fat in Agnes' food. Otherwise, I might worry," he added sarcastically.

"I promised myself I would only eat there once per week. It seems like I'm there every other day at least. I'm going to have to work on this some. I'll work out twice as hard today," Jamie suggested.

"It's going to take more than twice as hard for one day to get rid of this," Fred pointed out.

"Y'all stop," Em said as she entered the kitchen. "Just eat it and enjoy it." And they did just that.

Jamie told them about the library meeting/workshop on Thursday and her promise to join the Women's Club. They both agreed that joining the Women's Club could be good for business and commiserated with her for getting rooked into teaching the workshop. "I don't know. It might be fun. People always get excited about being able to get onto the Internet. I think I'll enjoy it."

"Oh, yeah," Fred said. "Junith and Mark are coming for dinner on Friday."

"Great, what do y'all want for dinner?" she asked.

"Fish or shrimp," Fred suggested. "How about that shrimp Creole casserole you make with hot peppers?"

"Okay. Sounds good. What about dessert?"

"I'll make dessert," Em proffered. "Maybe a chocolate cheesecake or rum pound cake with raspberries."

Jamie spent the afternoon preparing overheads and handouts for getting on the Internet. Once a teacher, always a teacher. She wrote out all of the instructions, step-by-step so the attendees could have a copy to keep. She used the color printer for the overheads. They looked great. She thought she might donate them to the library for later use.

Jamie exercised for forty minutes and swam a mile, guiltily. The boys sat with her by the pool for nearly half an hour before Jamie finally arose to take care of the kennel.

Jamie would need to deliver two guests home before 6 p.m. She bathed the two dogs, towel dried them and combed out their hair. Fred came in just as she was finishing up. "You had three calls: two for pick-ups tomorrow morning and one call from Junith." He looked at her gravely.

"What did Junith want?" Jamie asked.

"There was an accident on Highway 20. The driver of the mail truck was killed."

"You don't mean Tom," she whispered, scared to hear the truth.

"Yes. He ran off the road, but only after he was shot."

"Oh, Fred. His poor family. After all they put up with over the years."

"Junith said he was last seen talking with you outside of the post office."

Jamie explained to Fred what had happened. Fred said to call Junith and tell her. "I will but first I want to deliver these two guys home," Jamie said.

"I'll deliver them. You call Junith." Fred not so lovingly loaded the dogs into the truck and made his way down the driveway. She went inside to call Junith.

"Sheriff's Department," answered the voice said over the phone.

"Hey, Clyde. It's Jamie. Is Junith in?" she asked.

"No, she's still working the accident on Highway 20. Is there something I can do for you?" he asked.

"I just wanted to let you guys know that I talked to Tom just outside the post-office this morning around 11:30. He had entered the post-office to pick up the day's mail and make a delivery from Tallahassee. He had looked confused and mentioned in his words, "another overseas package?" I caught up with him outside and asked him what he was concerned about. He said there are packages to Washington, DC and Moscow weekly, and sometimes, daily."

There was silence at the other end of the line. "Clyde?"

"Yeah, I'm here. I'll pass this on to Junith. She will call you if she needs to talk to you."

"Thanks. Bye." As she hung up, Jamie realized she could hang around and be brutalized by Junith or she could get lost for a while. It was nearly 4 now.

"Em, want to go to a Women's Club meeting with me? Please!" she pleaded.

The look on her face was total disgust. "Okay, but only because you are a friend." They did not dress in cute little matching outfits with lots of accessories. Instead, they wore pants, albeit not jeans, shirts, not blouses, and jackets, not coats. They were subconsciously making a statement.

Jamie and Em arrived at the meeting just before they were ready to commence. Everyone was super nice to them. The asked about Em's experience but passed on asking about the accident and Tom.

"I'm so glad you both could make it," Mary Ann said. She had on a beaded necklace.

"What a pretty beaded necklace," Jamie complimented. "Where did you get it?" Em looked at Jamie like she was from outer space. The tone of her voice was not normal and the beads were outrageously ugly.

"Isn't it lovely? It's Russian. I bought it from Jim's Hardware store here in town. There were only a few."

They were introduced as new members and then sat back and listened. The meeting lasted about an hour. Jamie was impressed by the way the meeting was carried out. There was an agenda prepared in advance. Items were discussed and decided upon with great efficiency. The biggest item was the Winter

Festival, a yearly fund-raiser. The money was placed in the club treasury and disbursed based on need to families in the area. Last year, the fund-raiser produced $25,000. This year they hoped for an even better turn out. Everyone agreed to hold the fund-raiser two weeks before Christmas, a time most people are in a giving mood.

Once the agenda was completed, wine and cheese were served. Jamie and Em nibbled a bit and then politely excused themselves.

"Let's stop by the grocery store for some meat and veggies for sandwiches," Jamie suggested. Em rounded up the veggies while Jamie retrieved the turkey and fresh baked rolls. They met at the register in record time. "Want to stop by Joyner's for dessert?" Jamie asked as they walked out of the store.

Just as Em was about to reply, she looked up to see Junith leaning against the wall.

"Well, hello, Sheriff. How are you?" Jamie asked sweetly.

Junith coldly stared at her. "Y'all heading home?" she asked.

"Yes," Jamie lied. "Would you like to join us for sandwiches and a beer?"

"Okay. Go straight home," Junith commanded as she walked over to her car and drove off.

"What's wrong with her?" Em asked.

"PMS?" Jamie offered flippantly but she was clearly shaken.

Em glanced at Jamie and said, "I think I'll take my sandwich in my room when we get home."

Junith and Fred stood beside the Sheriff's car as Jamie and Em drove up. Even though Jamie had taken her time getting home, she still was not ready for the confrontation with Junith. But, her time was up. The four of them walked into the house together. Fred offered to layout the food for sandwiches and Em said she'd help. Junith and Jamie walked into the study to talk.

"Tell me about your meeting with Tom."

Jamie repeated everything she had told to Deputy Clyde. Junith stared at her while she talked, not moving a muscle and hardly blinking. It made Jamie nervous.

Finally she spoke. "Tom had started taking LSD again. His family doesn't know it. I found out from a friend on the force in Tallahassee who works undercover. His being dead is probably a blessing in disguise, if death ever can be."

This announcement took a tremendous burden off Jamie's shoulders. She had not wanted to admit nor even think that she had anything to do with Tom's death. Maybe it was a drug deal gone bad, or something.

Junith was reading Jamie's mind. "Jamie, you are not causing people to get killed. You seem to just be the last link before they get killed. I guess I could walk around with you for 24 hours a day to stop this mess."

"Then, we'd just kill each other," Jamie commented.

"That's the truth," she agreed and even smiled.

"Tammie was looking out of the window when I was talking to Tom. Think she had anything to do with it?" Jamie asked.

"Well, there's not much to do in that post office all day. I'd probably look out the window most of the time, too. I have talked to her. She had nothing to offer in the way of information. I can't arrest her for looking out of a window."

Junith rose to her feet and they headed into the kitchen. Fred and Em had everything ready. They ate basically in silence and then moved into the living room with wine and chocolate mints just as Deputy Clyde pulled in the driveway. Junith went out to meet him. They talked briefly as they made their way to the kitchen door.

"Wonder what's up?" Em asked.

Junith stuck her head in the door saying, "Thanks for supper. Gotta go." She walked swiftly back to her car and the two of them took off.

"We need to get a police radio," Jamie suggested.

"I wonder if they say anything worthwhile on the radio," Em put in. "Guys, I'm feeling better. If you don't mind, I'm going to try to get some work done. I'm a little behind."

"Great. I'll check the kennel for the night," Jamie offered.

"Guess that leaves me with the dishes," Fred added. Jamie just smiled and headed outside.

15

Everyone went his or her separate way on Wednesday. Fred organized his research so Jamie could enter the data sometime this week, Em worked at her computer, and Jamie prepared for the workshop for Thursday night.

For the workshop, she had several books that provided an index for the Internet searches, a list of businesses that would search for you, and a handout on how to access FreeNet. Her only fear was that she didn't have enough to keep them busy for half an hour.

Around 4:30 on Thursday, Jamie loaded her materials into the truck, and left Fred and Em to their work. Mrs. Swindemann was at the library. She had set up a TV connected to the computer so the audience could see the instructor's computer and be able to follow along. Again, Jamie was amazed at the library's technology and Mrs. Swindemann's technical abilities.

The librarian had placed a large piece of chart paper on the wall with directions on how to turn on the computer and get to the library home page. Jamie had planned to take them from the home page to the Internet to find places of interest and information on farming.

As it neared 5:30, the ten students began to arrive. JoAnn Reyner from the Women's Club was there, as was Mr. McNabb, Jim, the owner of the hardware store, and Shannon from the newspaper. The rest of the group was made up of teachers from the Junior High School. The principal required their attendance, evidently. That always made for an attentive group. Tammie was the last to arrive. She came empty handed and sat in the back of the room as Mrs. Swindemann introduced them and then turned it over to Jamie.

Teaching computer classes was always so aggravating. There are always a few people who started rushing through the assignment, which was fine, until they got stuck. Then, everyone had to stop and wait while someone got them back to where the rest of the class was. But, it is a good feeling to watch students get excited and become proficient in something they were scared to death to try before the class.

At the end of Jamie's thirty minutes, all ten students were surfing, laughing, and trying to outdo each other. Jamie bowed out and let Tammie carry on with her e-mail portion of the class.

Tammie had a cool demeanor but was very efficient in teaching e-mail. The students stayed up with her and did exactly what she said. They were successful in sending e-mail messages back and forth to each other. She asked if there were any questions. Jamie asked, "Is there a way to send a message without the receiver knowing who sent it?"

"Only if you use someone else's machine," she replied. No one else had any questions so Mrs. Swindemann went on to her portion of the class. Tammie and Jamie excused themselves.

"How about a cup of coffee, Tammie?" Jamie offered.

"I'm supposed to meet Eddie at Joyner's," she replied. "Would you like to join us for a drink?"

"Great." Jamie was shocked that she offered. Eddie was not at Joyner's when they arrived so Tammie and Jamie sat at the bar and drank coffee while talking about the workshop.

"Where did you learn so much about computers?" Jamie asked her.

"I taught myself, mainly. I enjoy using the machine and I like to use the Internet. I spend hours everyday on the computer," she admitted.

"Me, too." Out of the corner of her eye, Jamie saw Eddie enter the restaurant. She did not have time to pursue the mysterious e-mail with Tammie, now.

"Hello, ladies," Eddie said. "How was the workshop?"

"Hi, Eddie. Great. Tammie sure mesmerized them," Jamie offered.

Eddie just grinned and placed his hand on Tammie's shoulder. "Yeah, she's great," he said, smiling at her. Jamie excused herself.

Jamie was more tired than she thought. Once home, she worked in the kennel for a few hours before she let Minor and Major out for a quick romp before bringing them in for the night.

It was a beautiful night. The sky had cleared, the stars shone brightly, and a slight breeze blew cool, moist air. The night critters chirped away, and the owls called out. Jamie tucked all the dogs in, said good night and brought Major and Minor to the back porch with her. Major started to growl just before she got to the back door. Minor darted into the darkness, and barked wildly. Jamie ran to the back door and rushed in the house.

"The dogs are after something!" she said excitedly.

"Probably a stray dog. Don't be so edgy," Fred instructed. He walked to the back door to call the dogs but they were no where to be found. The barking had stopped. There was no movement and no sounds at all.

"That's strange. I guess they took off." They listened to the still night for several minutes.

"Fred, they have never taken off at night. They ran after something," Jamie said half angrily and half scared. "Let's go call them."

Just as they were about to step off of the deck, a shadow moved toward them. "Fred!" Jamie whispered. He pushed Jamie toward the porch, but neither of them moved quickly enough. A masked figure had a gun pointed at Fred and yelled for them to get back in the house. They moved in unison and did as they were told.

When they entered the house, the intruder turned out the kitchen lights before he entered. He was small, but the 9mm gun he carried looked large and deadly. Jamie looked over to Em's workplace. She was not there.

"Go into the living room and sit down on the couch," he said. The voice was familiar but he had a stocking over his face and his hair tucked into a baseball cap. The cap was familiar to Jamie. She recognized the baseball cap as the same one on the person attempting to mess with her truck at Joyner's a couple of weeks ago.

Again, they did as they were told. Jamie couldn't help but think what difference did it make who it was who held the gun that was going to kill her. She definitely knew they were going to be killed.

Just as the intruder moved them to the couch and pointed the gun at Fred's head, Fred jumped up and Em sprung out from behind the Lazy boy. The gun went off but it hit the ceiling instead of anybody. Fred and Em were all over the intruder. Jamie ran to the phone and dialed 911.

In the thirty seconds it took to tell what happened, Fred and Em had the intruder covered with her own gun. It was not a he. It was Tammie. "Where are my dogs," Jamie demanded. She looked at Jamie with disgust and spit at her face.

"I'm going to go look for the dogs," Jamie screamed to Fred and Em. She grabbed the fanny pack with the .38 and a flashlight and dashed out of the door.

"Jamie, come back here!" Fred yelled.

She ran in the direction from which Tammie had emerged. Screaming their names, with tears rolling down her eyes, she continued into the darkness. The tears increased. She just knew she was going to find them dead in a pool of blood. After 10 minutes, she heard the sirens coming into the driveway. She continued to search. After 5 minutes more, she heard Fred call. She continued to search, ignoring Fred's insistent calls. Just as she heard Fred yelling nearby and coming in her direction, Jamie saw the dogs. They were lying side by side in the bushes.

"Fred! Over here. I found them. Hurry. Over here!" She continued to holler so he could get the direction. Jamie ran up to them crying aloud now. "My boys are not dead," she kept saying aloud to herself. She knelt down beside them. "Over here, Fred!"

She felt for a pulse on Major. He was alive! And Minor, yes. He had a pulse too. "Fred!"

"Here I am, Jamie. How bad is it?" he asked.

"They are alive but I don't know what's wrong. Why are they just laying there?" She asked. "I don't see any bullet holes or blood."

"She must have thrown some food with drugs in it in order to quiet them. That's very generous of her, but she didn't want to shoot them and let us hear the shots."

"I can carry Minor. Can you lift Major?" she asked.

"No. Let me get some help. You stay here with them." He ran to the house and came back with a blanket and Deputy Clyde. Together they carried the big guy into the house while Jamie managed with Minor.

Tammie was gone by the time they got back to the house. Jamie was more interested in her dogs' health than what had happened to Tammie. Em had called Sandy Trevor, the vet, before taking off with Junith. He was on his way. They put Major and Minor on the couch, one at each end with their head directed at the middle. They looked so dead. They were totally limp.

The vet arrived. He looked at their eyes, and checked the vital signs. "Looks like they have been stunned. Their breathing is okay but they are in some sort of shock. Jamie sat in the middle with both heads in her lap.

Sandy looked at Jamie and said, "They will be fine. I'll take a blood sample to make sure. Just watch them tonight. If there is any change other than waking up hungry, let me know. Call me anytime."

"Thanks, Sandy. I appreciate your coming," Jamie said as he turned to leave. Fred walked him to his car.

"My poor babies." The tears were back. She patted their little heads and just cried. It was a release from all the action. By the time Fred got back, she was a mess. He brought her a cold wash cloth and a glass of ice water. It was exactly what she needed.

"So, what happened?" Jamie finally asked.

"Junith will be by as soon as she locks Tammie up. She will explain everything." Just as he said that, a Sheriff's car pulled up into the drive.

Junith and Em walked in. They looked at Jamie and then looked at Fred. The question in their eyes was "Are they dead?"

"The boys will be fine. They were hit with a stun gun," he explained.

Em grabbed a bottle of wine and four glasses. She poured as Junith began to explain.

"Tammie was recruited as a drug dealer by the Russian Mafia back in 1991. She was nurtured and educated to get a job with the US post office in DC. Once she had that post, they "waited" until something came open in a small town where she would be the only clerk. We are going to exhume Martin's body. While we all thought he had a heart attack while he was driving, it may be that he was taken out so this spot at the post office would be open for Tammie." They sipped their wine thinking about that one.

"Tammie's job has been to receive dope, powder cocaine and crack, to repackage it and send to the sellers, mainly in Tallahassee. She would receive the dope in Russian knickknacks. She would take the dope out, put it in boxes and send it to people in Tallahassee. Then, she would bundle the cash into a box and mail it back to Russia."

"Wasn't that a little risky, sending so much cash overseas?"

"Not really. Once in Russia, the Mafia contact picked it up at the airport. But Tammie thought she would make a little more on the side by selling the knickknacks. That was her downfall. We found traces of cocaine in the wooden dolls and other objects she sold through the hardware store," Junith explained.

"Did she kill Joe?" Fred asked.

"No, brace yourself for this. The person in charge of the drug dealing for the southeast is right here in Brookdale. The person who keeps track of the drugs brought in and cash received is our very own Ms. Swindemann, better known as Sanja in secret circles."

"What? I don't believe it," Jamie said.

"We picked her up last night for questioning. She sent you several e-mail messages and tried to convince us Mr. McNabb had sent them. She was contacted by the Mafia in 1989 and has been working for them ever since. She wanted to help the Mafia who in turned promised to help establish communism back in Russia. She's a commie down to her toes. She had Joe killed by one of her thugs because he had somehow figured out part of what was going on by talking to Tom. He thought he could make some money by blackmailing Tammie. He had no idea who he was really dealing with. She had some help to get rid of him, but I don't think we'll ever find out who."

"Did she drug me?" Em asked.

"No. You found that error on the corporate report. Jonathan Lime changed the numbers. He had encouraged his partners to make some investments that had gone bad and they did not want the stockholders to know. To make up for the losses, he convinced Smyth to rent his property out to a group of female Islamic militants for training purposes," explained Fred.

"Your trip from Egypt was very timely," Junith said to Fred.

"It was this group that kept trying to scare you off the property. Their encampment was just on the other side of the property line," Junith explained.

"Lime arranged for Em to be kidnapped so she could not bring up the change until he could fix it, and then blame her for the error," Junith continued. "I'm not sure we will ever be able to prove Lime actually had a part in it. He will probably walk away from this."

"Who brought me back then?" asked Em.

"The militants kept her drugged until he was ready to release her. Then, they deposited her at Eddie's, trying to make him look like the kidnapper. He got scared and put her in the kennel. He had put in the security system in the barn so he knew how to avoid it."

"So, is Eddie involved in all of this?" Em asked.

"Only minimally. He's down at the jail but we won't hold him. He had no idea about the drug smuggling ring. He is devastated that Tammie was involved.

"What about the fire in my kennel and the message on the door?"

"I think I may know who did both, but I'd rather wait until tomorrow for that one," Junith suggested.

"We can talk some more tomorrow. You and Mark come over for supper and we'll finish it the saga," Fred suggested.

"Junith, thanks for everything," Jamie said.

"Right. See ya."

Em, Fred and Jamie finished up the wine, opened another bottle of wine and finished it up. "I'm tired. See you two in the morning," Em said.

"Come on, Jamie. They will be fine. Let's get some sleep," Fred suggested.

"Okay, but leave the door open so I can hear them." She gave the each boy a kiss and a pet and left them for the night.

To her surprise, Jamie fell asleep immediately. She dreamt that she was washing her face, over and over for some reason. She opened her eyes to find Major and Minor licking her face while Fred and Em stood watching and laughing. She jumped up and hugged her boys.

"My babies are okay!" she exclaimed.

"Yes, and your babies probably need to go outside. I'll take them out while you shower and dress," Fred suggested.

"I'll fix breakfast," Em put in.

They sat down to their regular fare of peanut butter and jelly on whole wheat toast and coffee. "You know, now that everything is settled, it's time I moved back home," Em said.

"You know, Em. I had thought about taking one end of the barn and making an apartment out of it. If I remodeled the burned end, I can take it off my taxes. Would you be interested in renting it?" She held her breath for she could think of nothing better than having Em living in the kennel. Fred and Jamie had talked about it many times.

"I might. I just might. Let me think about it," she said.

"I'll do the dishes later. Leave them for now. Let's take a walk before you leave," Jamie suggested.

They donned their walking paraphernalia and took Major, Minor and Charlie. Out of habit, they headed down the path that led to the creek. There were three cars over on the property. They just had to go see what was up.

"Hello!" Some one waved from the Livingston property. It was Mary Ann, of all people.

"Hi, y'all. I wanted to introduce you to your new neighbor. This is Nathan Shoemaker. He is the CEO of Healthy Farms, Inc. This is Jamie Pellen and her husband Fred. And this is Em Rosini."

Nathan was 6'2", dark curly hair, the greenest eyes you've ever seen, olive skin and about 35 years old. "It is very nice to meet you all," he said to all of us but his eyes were on Em.

"Our pleasure," Jamie suggested. "Are you in town for a few days?" she asked.

"Just the weekend. I head back Sunday," he replied.

"Are you available for dinner tonight?" Jamie asked. "We are having a few friends over and would love to have you."

"That sounds super. What time?"

"Around 7:30. Casual so just come to relax," Jamie added.

"See you then." He still had not taken his eyes off of Em but waved and turned to walk the property with Mary Ann.

"Nice looking, huh, Em," Jamie suggested.

"Really, I hadn't noticed," she lied.

"Did you notice he didn't have a wedding band on?" Jamie teased.

"Yes," she admitted and they both broke out laughing.

"You noticed that?" Fred asked in amazement. "We men don't have a chance in this world."

After cleaning the kennel, Em and Jamie went to the store to get the supplies for dinner. Fred used the time to catch up on his writing. One of his textbooks was due for a revision and he was working on several articles, not to mention the project from Cairo.

Em prepared a rum cake with walnuts as Jamie peeled shrimp for the shrimp casserole. "What if Nathan doesn't eat shellfish or hot peppers?" she asked.

"Let him eat cake," Em smiled.

"Think I should go ahead and make it hot like we like it? Or, I could make a little one that is not hot," Jamie suggested.

"Naw. Let's break him into the real thing," she teased.

"Okay." She added 8 hot finger peppers to the frying pan and heated up the onions and cooked the shrimp. "It is hot," Jamie noted as she tasted it.

The afternoon went by quickly. Em and Jamie shared the duties of cleaning the house and working in the kennel, preparing dinner and setting the table. By 6:00 they were pooped. Fred came out of his study looking a little pooped, too. They changed for the arrival of their guests, that is they put on a pair of clean jeans, and decided to open a bottle of wine and relaxed. They had arranged for Junith and Mark to come an hour before Nathan so they could discuss last night's events in more detail. Junith and Mark arrived at 6:30 on the dot.

"Come on in. Good to see you again, Mark," Fred welcomed.

They stood in the kitchen. Jamie offered wine or beer. Both took wine. "So how is Brookdale's Russian druggie doing tonight?" Jamie asked.

"Neither Tammie nor Sanja are druggies. They never touched the stuff themselves. The story Tammie told the FBI is that the Mafia has her mother and father kidnapped in Moscow. Unless she did what Mrs. Swindemann AKA Sanja, told her, they threatened to kill them," Junith explained.

"Do you believe it?" Jamie asked.

"It doesn't matter to me," Junith said. "She broke the law here, no matter what the reason. I don't fall for that nonsense, personally. But, a jury would, if it could be proven. Anyway, it is out of my hands. They were both hauled away by the FBI."

"What about the kennel fire?" Fred asked.

"I took care of that this morning. It was Mr. McNabb. He was mad that you wouldn't board his dog. He confessed the only reason he wanted to board the dog was to get inside your kennel to look at it to see why people boarded their dogs with you. He has a kennel in Tallahassee and was ticked off because some Tallahasseeans would bring their dogs all the way to you instead of to him. He had tried to undersell you, bad-mouth you, and then tried to burn your kennel down to stop the competition. He set up that appointment to board his dog so he could check you out. He never had any intention of really leaving that Pitbull with you."

"Sounds like a nut to me," Jamie said.

"He's been charged with arson. We cannot hold him and he'll just get a fine since nothing was damaged much," Junith explained. "He did admit to sending you one e-mail message. He wanted to scare you. He had no idea you were getting other messages from Tammie. She sent hers from the post office. He sent his from the library."

Headlights appeared in the driveway. It was a Toyota Land Cruiser. "Hey, Em. At least he has a practical vehicle," Jamie teased. She looked out of the window, too.

"Not bad," she said.

Nathan came to the door in jeans and a red and black checked flannel shirt with casual hiking boots. He was welcomed as he presented two bottles of red zinfandel. "We are all anxious to hear about your company, Nathan," Fred said opening up the topic for conversation.

"Well, things are moving rapidly. Hopefully, we can be in business by this time next year," he said. "I am particularly excited to see you have a kennel right next door. I raise Aussie Shepherds to show."

"Really? I have an Aussie. Want to see him?" Jamie asked.

"Sure," he responded. What else could he say? Jamie went out to get Minor from the pen.

"Now, here is a show dog," Jamie said as Minor nip kissed her on the ear.

"He really is beautiful. He definitely has strong tri-colored markings. Let me see his teeth." Nathan looked at his teeth, felt his hair and watched him walk. He is show quality. Let me know if you want to enter him in a show," he said graciously.

"Just out of curiosity, Nathan, what do you plan to farm next door?" Fred asked.

"Portebello mushrooms, alfalfa sprouts, and hydroponic tomatoes are our specialties," he replied.

"Is this your first farming business adventure?" Jamie asked.

"No. I have several farms out west. A few years ago, I had planned to open one in central Florida. My wife had family in the area. Just after we purchased the land and put in a road, she was killed in a car accident," he said quietly, the hurt still apparent in his eyes.

"I'm sorry," Jamie said.

"Me, too. After 3 years, I've learned to go on with my life but it was rough going for awhile. A drunk fell asleep at the wheel and hit her head on. She died instantly. I just couldn't continue there. Too many bad memories. I put the land up for sale and looked around until I found this acreage. I traded that property plus $500 per acre for this land."

"Why did you need so much wooded land for your farm?" Em asked.

"I like this area. I'm going to build my home here and make this my headquarters."

The hot and spicy shrimp casserole was enjoyed by all. It turned out that Nathan loved the hot peppers. Em's dessert was a big hit.

She covered the walnut rum cake with raspberries and whipped cream. Loud talk and laughter could be heard until late in the night. It was a great way to release the anxiety that had built up over the last month.

Fred and Jamie made reservations for the beach, but only after she had entered his Egyptian data in the computer. Em agreed to move above the kennel so she was left to design her apartment. Eddie was going to do the carpentry work, including a sprinkler system.

Jamie sat on the deserted sand dunes at St. George Island watching Fred swim far out into the Gulf. Her mind was rushing over the events for the past few weeks, trying to sort out the happenings. Suddenly a Turkish saying popped into her mind. "One day older, a year wiser." She felt more like one year older and one day wiser. Shaking her head as if to clear it, she walked to the water's edge and plunged into the rolling surf.

About the Author

Princess Palmer is a native Floridian who has traveled extensively in the Middle East. She works to incorporate the exotic settings from her travels with the splendors found in the wilds of North Florida. She presently resides in Beirut, Lebanon.